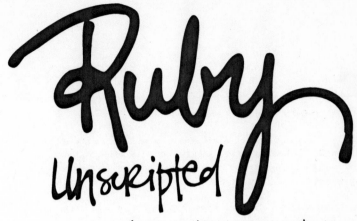

Ruby

Unscripted

life is what happens when
you lose the script

CINDY MARTINUSE...

THOMAS NELSON
Since 1798

NASHVILLE DALLAS MEXICO CITY RIO DE JANEIRO BEIJING

Published in Nashville, Tennessee. Thomas Nelson is a trademark of Thomas Nelson, Inc.

Thomas Nelson books may be purchased in bulk for educational, business, fund-raising, or sales promotional use. For information, please e-mail SpecialMarkets@ThomasNelson.com.

Publisher's Note: This novel is a work of fiction. Names, characters, places, and incidents are either products of the author's imagination or used fictitiously. All characters are fictional, and any similarity to people living or dead is purely coincidental.

Published in association with Books & Such Literary Agency, Janet Kobobel Grant, 52 Mission Circle, Suite 122, PMB 170, Santa Rosa, CA 95409-5370

Library of Congress Cataloging-in-Publication Data

Martinusen-Coloma, Cindy, 1970–
  Ruby unscripted / Cindy Martinusen-Coloma.
    p. cm.
  Summary: When fifteen-year-old Ruby, along with her mother, stepfather, and younger brother, move to Marin County, California, leaving her older brother back home with her father and stepmother, she feels lost among the wealthier, more sophisticated people she meets, but gradually she begins to see a side of herself that never really fit into her old life, and she opens herself up to the new experiences that God is offering her.
  ISBN 978-1-59554-356-1 (softcover)
  [1. Moving, Household—Fiction. 2. Divorce—Fiction. 3. Interpersonal relations—Fiction. 4. Family life—California—Fiction. 5. Identity—Fiction. 6. Motion pictures—Production and direction—Fiction. 7. Christian life—Fiction. 8. Marin County (Calif.)—Fiction.] I. Title.
  PZ7.M36767Ru 2009
  [Fic]—dc22   2009002382

Printed in the United States of America
09 10 11 12 RRD 6 5 4 3 2 1

For and inspired by Madelyn Rose

chapter one

"*Now* he likes me?" I say aloud as I drop my phone to my lap and my heart does a strange little tuck and roll within my chest.

My ten-year-old brother, Mac, gives me a strange look from the seat beside me. With the top down in my aunt's convertible, he can't hear my words that are cast into the air to dance with the wind.

The orange towers of the Golden Gate Bridge loom toward us, with the darkening blue of sky and water filling the spaces between. Aunt Jenna is driving, with Mom talking beside her.

So it's finally true.

Nick likes me.

I think I'm happy. Everyone will expect me to be happy. It's not been a secret that I've liked him for . . . well, ever. Or at least for a few months.

And yet I have a very good reason for being completely annoyed about this.

The text stating Nick's indirect admission of love, or at least "like," arrives as we're leaving an afternoon in San Francisco behind. But we aren't driving the four hours home to Cottonwood. We're driving toward our new life in Marin County.

Everyone at school knew that Nick liked me for a long time. His friends and my friends knew it. I knew it. But Nick apparently didn't know his own feelings. Why can't guys just trust others on these things?

I pick up my phone and reply to Kate's text.

ME: Is Nick still standing there?

KATE: No. I think it freaked him out to wait for your response. The guys went to play Alien Hunter III before the movie starts. So what do you think? Patience paid off.

ME: I'm trying not to think that guys are really as dumb as most of us say they are.

KATE: Huh?

ME: Really now. I mean NOW. He says this on the day I move away?

KATE: Well you'll be home most every weekend so it's not that bad.

ME: But think about it. What made him decide today?

KATE: Who cares? He finally figured out he can't live without you.

The car cruises along the bridge, and I stare up at the massive orange beams over our heads. Then I catch sight of a sailboat as it dips and bows on the evening waters of San Francisco Bay.

My brother is shout-talking to my mom and aunt. And with one earbud pulled out, I catch bits of the discussion being tossed around the car as the wind twists my hair into knots. The topic is "If you had one wish, what would you wish for?"

What poetic irony. Five minutes ago I would've wished that Nick would like me . . . and like some psychic genie working even before I wished it, the text arrived from Kate: "Nick said . . ."

So Nick likes me *after* I move four hours and a world away.

He likes me the day *after* I say good-bye to him and all my friends in Cottonwood.

I scroll back through my saved texts to find what he sent me after we said good-bye.

NICK: I wish you weren't moving.
NICK: Next time you're up visiting your dad let's hang out.
NICK: How often will you be back?
NICK: So you don't have a date for prom?

Men. I mean seriously.

So it's like this. I'm moving to one of the coolest areas of California—Marin County. I'm going to live in this cool, quirky cottage that my aunt Betty gave us after she headed off on an extended Mediterranean honeymoon with the man, now her husband, she found online.

Since I was a little girl, I've wanted to live near San Francisco. Aunt Betty's house was one of my favorite places. Kate and I plan to attend college down here. So now I get to live my dream sooner than expected.

Mac taps my arm, but I watch the little sailboat lean toward the open Pacific and wonder at its journey ahead, far or near, some California marina or faraway exotic isle.

My brother taps on my arm persistently. "Ruby-Ruby Red."

I really dislike it when he calls me that. Then he reaches for my earbud, and I push his hand away.

"What?" I ask loudly, wiping strands of hair from my face. The sun falls easily into the cradle of the sea. It's eventide—that time between sunset and darkness, a peaceful time of wind and bridges and dreams except for one annoying brother and an incoming text that could disrupt the excitement of a dream coming true.

"What do *you* wish for?" Mac asks earnestly.

My phone vibrates again, and I nearly say, "Don't bug me, and don't call me Ruby-Ruby Red," but Mac's sweet pink cheeks and expectant eyes stop me. I rub his hair and tickle him until he cries for mercy.

He laughs and twists away from my fingers, then asks me again what I wish for.

"Wait a minute," I say, and he nods like he understands.

KATE: He said he's been miserable since he said good-bye
    last night.
ME: So why didn't he like me before?
KATE: He says he always did, he just kept it to himself.
ME: Or he kept it FROM himself.

Everyone said Nick said I was hot, that I was intelligent, that he'd never met a girl like me—which can be taken as good or bad. Everyone told him to ask me out, but he just didn't. No explanation, no other girlfriend, just nothing. For months. Until today.

KATE: He's never had a girlfriend, give the guy a break. I
    always thought he'd be the bridge guy! Maybe he will be!

I rest the phone in my hands at that. Nick has been the main character in my bridge daydream—only Kate knows that secret dream of mine.

We've crossed the bridge into Marin County with signs for Sausalito, Corte Madera, San Rafael. The names of my new home, and yet I'm still between the old and the new.

"What are you smiling for?" my brother asks.

"Nothing," I say and give him the mind-your-own-business look.

Mac stretches forward in his seat belt toward the front seat, and I'm tempted to tell him to sit down. But for once I don't boss him around. He's so happy about this wishing talk, with his wide dimpled smile and cheeks rosy from the wind. His cheeks remind me of when I loved kissing them—back when we were *much* younger.

"Remember, no infinity wishes. That's cheating," Mac shout-says to Mom and Aunt Jenna, but he glances at me to see if I'm listening.

"This is really hard," Aunt Jenna yells back. She points out the window to a line of cyclists riding along a narrow road parallel to the highway. "I bet those guys wish for a big gust of wind to come up behind them."

Mac laughs, watching the cyclists strain up an incline.

Now they'll probably start "creating wishes" for everyone they see.

I bet that car wishes it were as cool as that Corvette.

I think the people in that car wish they had a fire extinguisher for that cigarette . . .

Mom and her sister often make up stories about strangers

while sitting outside Peet's Coffee or, well, just about anywhere people watching is an option.

My phone vibrates in my hand, and then immediately again.

KATE: Hello?? No comment on Nick being your mysterious
    bridge guy?
ME: Nope
JEFFERS: So beautiful, are you there yet?
ME TO KATE: I just got a text from Jeffers.
KATE: LOL He's sitting beside me and saw me talking to you.
JEFFERS: When can we come party in Marin?
ME TO JEFFERS: Almost there. Ten minutes I think. Uh party?
JEFFERS: Yeah, party! How could you leave us, I mean
    what could be better than us? You'll be too cool for
    gocarts and mini golf after a month w/ the rich and
    sophisticated.
ME: I hate mini golf.
JEFFERS: See? One day and already too good for mini golf.
KATE: You're having us all down for a party?
ME: Uh, no
JEFFERS: Kate's yelling at me. Thx a lot. But bye beautiful,
    previews are on with little cell phone on the screen
    saying to turn you off.
ME TO JEFFERS AND KATE: K have fun. TTYL.
KATE: Write you after. Bye!

It's a significant moment, this.
One of the most significant in my fifteen years.
Not the "wish discussion" between Mac, Mom, and Aunt

6

Jenna; not the text messaging back and forth; not the music play-ing in one of my ears; not even Nick liking me.

The significance comes in crossing bridges. Not the bridge in my dream, but the ones that take me into Marin. The many bridges that brought my family here with my dad still in Cottonwood, and my older brother, Carson, driving soon behind us. And though we can turn around and drive back to the small town I've always lived in, I wonder if, once you cross so many bridges, you can ever really go back.

The music in my one ear and the voices of my family in the other make a dramatic backdrop for this moment—one that will shape the rest of my life.

I feel a sense of wonder, but also of fear. It's beautiful, this time of long evening shadows. The sky in the west where the sun has fallen turns from a subtle to defined sunset of red and orange. The hills of Marin County rise to the nighttime with their myriad dots of light. The salty breeze is cool coming off the Pacific.

"What's your wish?"

I jump as Mac shouts at me, leaning to get his face close to mine. I nearly throw my phone out the open rooftop.

"Mac! Mom!"

"Mac, leave your sister alone. She needs time to think," Mom calls back with a worried glance in my direction.

She was more worried than I was about this move to Marin . . . well, until I said all the good-byes this week and especially now. I realize it's the last remnant of what is, taking us from the past and *what has been* to the new place, the new life, and the *what will be.*

"Do you know what I wish?" Mac says in a loud whisper that only I can hear.

The innocent expression on his face soothes my annoyance. He motions for me to lean close.

"I wish I was six again."

"Why?"

"Promise you won't tell Mom or Austin or Dad and Tiffany, 'cause I don't want to hurt their feelings . . ." He waits for me to agree. "I wish I was six 'cause Mom and Dad were married then. But then that would make Austin and Tiffany go away, and I don't really want them to go away, but I sort of wish Mom and Dad were married still."

I nod and glance up toward Mom, who is staring out toward the bay. "Yeah, I know, Mac. But it'll be all right."

"So what do you wish for?" he asks again.

We're almost there now, and I still have no singular wish. How do you make such a choice when your whole life is upended—for the good and the bad? I wonder if San Francisco Bay is like one giant wishing well, and in the coming years I can toss as many pennies as I want into the blue waters and have all the wishes I need.

I hope so. And maybe wishing that the bay would become one giant well breaks Mac's rule about infinity wishes. But regardless, this is what I wish my wish to be.

It was my choice to move to Marin with Mom. But now I wonder if these bridges are taking me where I should be going. Or if they're taking me far, far away.

"I wish for infinity wishes!" I say and kiss Mac on the cheek before he protests. "No one can put rules on wishes."

And this is what I truly want to believe.

chapter two

"Aunt Betty's house is kind of creepy at night," Mac says as the car makes a turn up the driveway and the two-story house comes into view.

"It isn't Aunt Betty's house anymore," I say, thinking how right Mac is.

The lights from the upstairs windows stare down at our approach. I see Austin and Uncle Jimmy carrying my dresser through the garage, and they set it down as our headlights blind them.

"Okay, then *our* house is kind of creepy at night." Mac's jaw is set in a way that says, *I'm too big to be a chicken*, but his eyes are wide and dart around the thick trees, ferns, and bushes that encroach the property. "Ruby," he whispers. "Do you think the house is haunted?"

"No."

"Promise?" His eyes look to me for reassurance.

"Yes, I promise."

Aunt Betty's house, built in the early 1900s, is the coolest place I've ever seen. It has two secret-looking doors—one in the parlor by the fireplace and another in a room upstairs—that go into boxlike storage areas.

When my brother Carson was six, he broke his arm going down the laundry chute that slides from the second story down to the basement. His teddy didn't break its arm when it went down the chute, Carson cried, so why did he?

And, of course, just having a basement is a rare and exciting thing in California. Aunt Betty converted it from a cold, damp space into an entertainment room with books, puzzles, games, a TV, and a DVD player. Supposedly, a movie director owned the house in the forties, but I can't remember who it was or what movies he made. The yard reminds me of *The Secret Garden*. Carson and I have spent hours exploring and playing there.

But Mac is right—tonight with the garden shadows leaning in and the house so full of old stories, it appears downright creepy.

Uncle Jimmy and Austin wave with gloves on their hands. The moving truck is gone, but boxes and furniture fill the garage and driveway close to the house. Aunt Jenna pulls to a stop and turns off the engine as the guys come toward us.

"Here we are," Austin says.

Austin is my stepdad of six months. He leans into the open car and kisses Mom before opening her door. He says hi to me and rubs Mac's hair, eliciting a "Hey, not the hair"—something the two of them say often.

"Do you think the house is haunted, Austin?" Mac asks in a whisper, as if the ghosts might overhear him.

"I've been here all day, and no sign of anything."

"But that was daytime."

"When your mom and I came down to paint and get the house ready, there were no ghosts then either."

Uncle Jimmy gives me a wide smile. "Hey, you just missed Kaden."

"We did?" my aunt says, and now they're all smiling at me. "You were supposed to keep him here."

"Yeah. Strangely, when I mentioned my fifteen-year-old niece that we wanted him to meet, he had to get going."

"What are you guys talking about?" I ask.

"We want you to meet Kaden," Mom says. "Don't you remember, I mentioned him?"

"Uh, no." But then I do vaguely remember some mention of a guy, though it's not unusual for Mom to have some "nice young man" to introduce me to. They're usually from church, or the nice fella who takes her groceries to her car. My parents, stepparents, and other relatives do these matchmaking things—but then don't actually want me dating anyone. This is my observation anyway.

"Oh, Ruby, you're going to like Kaden."

Aunt Jenna has a pretty convincing expression, and I do trust her judgment a bit more than Mom's—though I'm not sure why.

"He's been helping with some yard work, and today he helped unload the heavy furniture."

"A yard guy? Interesting."

"No, he's really cute," Aunt Jenna says, and Mom nods her head.

"And he's really hot," Austin says with a laugh. "Or at least you'll think so. Actually, I didn't like him at first."

"You didn't?" Mom and Aunt Jenna say together.

"I didn't either," Uncle Jimmy says.

"Why?" we all ask.

"He's one of those silent and suspicious guys," Uncle Jimmy explains, and I instantly imagine a serial killer.

Austin nods, and I wonder why we're having this long conversation about the yard boy when we've just arrived at our new house.

"He didn't talk a lot. But then once you're around him awhile, he's really great."

Aunt Jenna closes the car door. "Something tragic happened in his family, I heard. I don't know what."

That makes everyone quiet until Mac yells from the house, "Hey, I got the green room with the secret closet, right?"

"Yes, Mac," Mom says, and we start moving toward the house, finally. "And sorry, Ruby, but your room is still a mess."

"Which room did I end up with?" I glance at the apartment over the garage that's Carson's room, the one I wanted.

Aunt Betty used to rent it out to college students. It has a small kitchen and an old cast-iron bathtub and walk-in tile shower. I'm counting the years till Carson moves out. Kate and I might stay there when we go to college.

We walk through the garage and into the small kitchen with the new, light-colored granite that brightens up the dark wood cabinets and tile floor. "Wow, this looks nice."

"Isn't it beautiful?" Mom smiles proudly. "And your room has newly refinished floors. We thought you'd want Aunt Betty's, since it has its own bathroom and the little balcony."

"It does? Sweet," I say. "My memories are of a flower infusion and the smell of old lady and wet dog."

Mom knows I can't stand bad smells. There's a restaurant back home that smells so strongly of fish, I can't walk in the door. And I'm not completely opposed to fish usually.

"We took down the old wallpaper and painted it. It doesn't smell like wet dog anymore, and only slightly of old lady." Mom smiles. "Just kidding. It smells of paint and floor lacquer, but that'll clear out soon." Now Mom has her convincing expression and twinkle in her blue eyes—*Everything is going to be okay, you'll see.* "We'll have gas for the furnace and phone and Internet access tomorrow."

"Tomorrow?" A panic rises in my chest as we stand in the kitchen between boxes. I need to get online tonight. Where is my phone charger?

"We all might sleep in the living room tonight, by the fire-place. It gets pretty cold at night. Aunt Jenna and Uncle Jimmy are staying over too. It'll be a slumber party."

Mac somehow overhears this from upstairs and yells, "Slumber party! Slumber party!"

"Great," I say dully. Why did we come down tonight instead of staying in Cottonwood if the house wasn't ready? Or I could've stayed at Kate's. Then I would've been at the movies with everyone and heard Nick's admission in person. Though he may have said it only because I'm gone.

Mom goes upstairs to join Aunt Jenna and Mac in his room, and the men have retreated back to the garage to put things together. The sounds of my family fade beneath the dull silence of the house. It's cold and empty and smells of paint and that strange mustiness of homes near the ocean.

I see a framed Monet print sitting on the floor by the cold

13

fireplace, propped against the wall. It's the garden scene in hues of blue that hung in the house we lived in for ten years. The house we lived in with Dad and Mom together. Now it's going to hang in Aunt Betty's house.

Suddenly everything feels awkward, and a shiver goes down my spine. I wonder where Dad is right now, and how soon until Carson arrives. Maybe he and I can take a drive tonight, go to Dutch Bros. or explore the winding hillside roads that connect the towns of Marin. To our west is San Francisco Bay; our little town of Corte Madera climbs up the mountain, and on the other side of the peak is the wide Pacific. South is the Golden Gate and San Francisco, and north is Santa Rosa and the California wine country. I think of this and imagine exploring the roads and ocean inlets. Carson needs to hurry up and get here.

My friends said I was lucky to move from Cottonwood to Aunt Betty's old house in Marin. I agreed. But as I ascend the steps to my new bedroom with a coldness going deep into my skin, I wonder if this move is really so great after all.

I carry my phone up the narrow stairway to Aunt Betty's room—my room—which is off to the right at the top of the stairs. The rest of the rooms go toward the left, so that's another plus—a bit of privacy at this end of the house, no one complaining about my music being too loud the way they did at the rented house we've stayed in since the divorce.

Standing in the entrance of my new domain, which is bigger than I remember, I look over the hardwood floors. They do shine nicely. The plaster walls look better with a cream-colored paint. The ceiling has thick dark wood and beams, a perfect place for strings of lights or paper lanterns. With all the boxes, it's a maze to walk through. My full-sized mattress is in the corner, up against the wall. It reminds me of a room you might see in one of those old movies Mom and I like to watch—*Casablanca* or something. That makes me like it better.

Mom said I could bring the old phonograph to my room, and I imagine painting on the balcony with the grainy sounds of a Billie Holiday record playing in the background. Aunt Betty's massive rolltop desk is in one corner. I'd forgotten about it. It too fits the 1940s classic feel. I have to use two hands to lift the cover, but then it slides easily back. A note and new journal rest on the smooth wood desktop.

> *To my dear Ruby, the new occupant of my beloved room.*
> *Dream big dreams! Work hard to attain them! Look how even an old woman like me can have dreams come true. By the time you read this, I will be dancing in Madrid with Herbert.*
> *See you in a few months.*
>
> *Hasta la vista—*
> *Aunt Betty*

Beneath the note is an article Mom wrote for a singles magazine. She writes so many articles, I didn't even know she'd written one about Aunt Betty. It's titled "Love in Cyberspace" and is about Internet matchmaking success stories. The main photograph is of Aunt Betty with Herbert kissing her cheek.

I imagine feisty Aunt Betty on her long honeymoon with Herbert—Uncle Herbert, as he's now officially named. Uncle

Herbert appeared to be about as exciting as a zombie. But then he surprised everyone at their wedding when he and Aunt Betty performed a perfect and impressive tango.

Right now they might be dancing at a fiesta with Aunt Betty wearing a flowery old-lady hat—who wears things like that anymore? Aunt Betty does.

I hear Mac calling me from downstairs. He calls and calls even after I respond with a "What?" Finally he races up and into my room.

"We're having a campout in the living room!"

"Yes, and for a ten-year-old, this is the best thing in the world."

"You don't think it's fun? Austin's going to get Chinese food and stuff to make s'mores in the fireplace."

"Oh yeah, I'm stoked," I lie.

"It'll be like when we went camping at Patrick's Point."

"Except that we're in a house, and we won't be cooking over a campfire or walking on the beach at night. And we don't have Dad or Carson."

"Yeah," he says, and the fun fizzles right out of his expression, which makes me feel the big g-u-i-l-t-y.

As much as Mac loves Austin and Dad's wife, Tiffany, and it's been four years since our parents lived together, he continually brings up memories of times with Dad. He forgets that Mom and Dad had a big fight on that trip to Patrick's Point. Dad and Carson went fishing for the day, and Mom took Mac and me shopping, and neither spoke more than a few words on the drive home. Fun trip.

"I was going to make a tent where my bed is."

"Mac," I say as he leaves the room in the exact opposite mood he came in with. "I'll make a s'more with you."

That brings the big wide smile that could seriously put the kid in commercials. "Okay! See you downstairs. And you need to see my secret compartment in my room."

I stay in my new room until the cold seeps in from outside and the shivers take over.

There are mattresses all over the living room and a fire blazing so hot that everyone sits without jackets. I peel mine off as I enter the room.

So here we are.

And then Mom's cell phone rings.

chapter three

I listen to Mom on the phone with a sinking feeling in my stomach. It's not that hard to figure out that someone is dead, and then a few moments later who that person is.

When someone dies, it's like everything you know about them and any memories you have all become heightened and important. I didn't know Tony Arnold all that well.

"How did it happen?" Mom says, sitting on the edge of a large cardboard box.

We gather around her to hear the tragic details.

"That's horrible."

Though we weren't close friends, Little Tony, as everyone called him, and I went to church together for years. We were in Sunday school and youth group. We were in the Christmas play every year. He was a grade older but looked years younger.

"I'll send Maggie some flowers," Mom says, referring to Tony's mother, before ending the conversation.

"Little Tony Arnold is dead? What happened?" Aunt Jenna asks before I do.

"It's so awful. He overdosed."

"Sweet little Tony?" Aunt Jenna asks, and it is hard to think of him as anything but that cute little guy we knew at church.

I remembered once during church when Little Tony and I were supposed to help in children's church, but instead we went exploring. We heard a noise and raced through a door, with Little Tony going first. He fell straight into the baptismal during the pastor's sermon. I could laugh at the memory, except that now Tony is dead.

"I guess he's been doing a lot of drugs and drinking a lot."

And there is talk about it for a while, and discussion of how sad it all is, but then everyone moves on after the arrival of the Chinese food and the search for a few more sleeping bags. But I can't stop thinking of little Tony Arnold. It's like he lingers on the borders of everything we do and say.

Kate texts me awhile later when we're all in our sleeping bags. Mac is playing his Nintendo DS under his covers. I'm texting friends.

KATE: Hey.

ME: This kid I knew died.

KATE: Who?

ME: I don't think you know him. He went to my church.
　　　Little Tony we called him.

KATE: Well, that's a name to haunt a guy. How'd he die?

ME: That's the crazy part. Drugs. He was this sweet
  little kid. I saw him last Christmas. He was still
  really short and cute.
KATE: Short and cute? Named Little Tony, and he's in high
  school?
ME: Yeah, which would be painful.
KATE: Guess that explains the drugs.
ME: Yeah. Maybe.

And I can't stop thinking of him. Every memory I can resurrect, I find and go over, searching for some hint of the shortness of his life. Little weird things like a funny story he told on a youth trip to Marine World, or how when we watched the movie *Simon Birch*, the main character reminded us of Little Tony. Things like that.

And I don't want to forget him, which is strange. How often have I ever thought of him except when I'd see him? Now I can't stop thinking about him. Because now he's dead. Little Tony is dead, and isn't it important to remember him now, to give some kind of meaning to his life?

It's midnight, and I'm texting from inside my sleeping bag with the phone charger plugged into the wall.

KATE: Nick asked me what you said.
ME: What I said?
KATE: About him liking you. I told him the movie started
  so I didn't get a reply.
ME: What is this, seventh grade? He can't ask me these
  things himself?

This Nick drama is annoying me, probably because I'm moody and antsy and want Carson to get here. He should hear about Little Tony, who was a grade in between us. Carson will remember the time Little Tony did a perfect rendition of an Oompa-Loompa from *Charlie and the Chocolate Factory*.

KATE: Well, it is Nick. He either has a girl calling and
      chasing him, or he doesn't really know what to do.

I like this guy, I remind myself. In between the other guys I've liked, Nick has been on the top five list for maybe two years, moving into the number one slot in the past months. We danced once at a freshman orientation dance—one of our friends forced us together—and for a split second I thought he might kiss me. Then someone bumped into us, and the magic was gone. Our friends said we'd make the best couple; we even look alike in a way. We both have dark hair and blue eyes, complexions that tan easily, and he's enough inches taller that I wouldn't tower over him in heels.

Uncle Jimmy keeps snoring off and on.

Aunt Jenna hits him and whispers, "You're snoring again. Roll over." There's some scuffling around, and then he rolls over.

KATE: You still awake?
ME: Of course
KATE: Allen wants me to play Xbox.
ME: Let me guess. His friends are gone so he's begging
     little sister.
KATE: You know it. He really needs to go back to college.

My parents are bout to go crazy. But why so little talk
bout Nick? I'm starting to think you don't like him.

ME: I do. Just being down here now, knowing it's for real,
and then hearing about that kid dying . . .
everything's weird. I should just force myself to
sleep.

KATE: Wish you were here eh?

ME: Yeah

I want to write, *But this is my chance, the change I've wanted
for years.*

Near the city I can explore art and culture. It's sort of been
my dream, if I really knew what my dreams were. I've just known
that I wanted something different. Most of my friends wouldn't
ever guess—how something feels wrong at times, sometimes
during the strangest moments like the middle of class or during
a dance or while sitting around talking to everyone. Mom would
say it's because I have a sense of purpose and calling for my life.
Uh-huh. Aunt Jenna would say no one feels like they fit in during high school.

All I know is the essence of my dreams, and this awkward
"nonfitting" feeling. I want to do things and see places that I can't
quite put into words.

KATE: LOL. No, you don't really want to be here. You've
stared out the windows for too many years my friend.

ME: What?

How does she know about this?

Ruby Unscripted

KATE: Don't you remember in seventh grade?

ME: What in seventh grade?

KATE: Mr. Quigley called you a zoner cause you were
   always staring out the windows. I asked why you
   didn't concentrate better. We were at the picnic
   tables at lunch. I remember perfectly.

ME: Remember what?

KATE: You said you were imagining the day when you escaped
   our little town. I said that I liked our little town. We got in
   a big fight about it. We didn't talk till the next day.

ME: We didn't?

KATE: I can't believe you don't remember.

ME: I don't.

KATE: You said don't take it wrong. You had nothing against
   our little cow town. Which of course made me mad
   again. I said what was wrong with a cow town?

ME: I remember. We laughed that you called it a cow
   town too, but didn't like ME saying it.

KATE: Yes! The fight was over. But you said you wanted to
   explore the world, do something exciting.

ME: I was like that back then?

KATE: Oh, even earlier! In kindergarten you told Mrs K
   you were going to be Van Gogh. So see? You're doing
   what you've dreamed.

ME: I guess so

KATE: Don't let it get messed up.

Uncle Jimmy is back to snoring. I lie there for a long time,
wishing one of my friends would pop in to say hello. Uncle Jimmy

snorts a loud one, and I hear a snicker across the room, then Mac's whisper: "Is anyone else awake?"

"Yes," I whisper back.

"Yes," say my mom, Aunt Jenna, and Austin in unison.

For some reason, this makes Mom and Aunt Jenna start laughing. It infects us all, and soon we laugh so hard that Uncle Jimmy wakes in panic.

"What's going on? What's happening?"

Which makes us laugh harder, of course.

It's four o'clock, and we all get up. Mom digs through boxes for paper plates, the griddle, and pancake mix and starts mixing waffles while Austin makes coffee.

"Oh my gosh," Aunt Jenna says, jumping up like the house is on fire. "Tomorrow is Thursday? I mean, today is Thursday the twenty-first. Oh, I can't believe it. With all the details of the move, I totally forgot, and we are definitely not ready."

We're all asking, "What, what?"

"It's Premiere Night tomorrow. I mean today."

"Oh no," Mom says.

"Didn't Terri go on that health-spa vacation?" Uncle Jimmy asks, he too seeing this as a grave situation, and I want to interrupt and ask what Premiere Night is.

"Yes." Aunt Jenna rubs her neck, a worried expression on her face.

She owns a coffeehouse/cinema called the Underground. I'm supposed to start working there next week.

"I could start tomorrow," I say. "Or today, that is."

At first Aunt Jenna protests, but she needs me. And so I'll be starting work at eleven.

"Oh, it looks like your brother left a message last night. Your dad said he was having trouble with the truck," Mom says as she punches in numbers on her cell phone.

Again? I thought he'd be here already. It's like my wings are clipped with him gone. It's Thursday, and since Mom isn't making us start school till Monday, I'm thinking we could explore half of Marin County.

"Ruby, will you take over the waffles?"

Mom walks out of the kitchen before I respond. Austin follows her.

Maybe Carson can pick me up after work. He may grumble and complain about taking me places, but unless he's heading off with his friends, he usually goes where I want to go. And down here, he won't have friends at first. He'll want to do things with me even more—

Mom returns to the kitchen all quiet and distracted-like.

"Did Carson say when he'll be here?" I ask.

Mom is silent long enough to make me stare at her, ignoring the waffle sizzling in the iron.

"What? What is it?"

"He's not coming. It sounds like he wants to live with your dad."

chapter four

Carson not living with us?

Not here to drive me around or talk to or even to fight with?

Then the full impact hits me. I might be going to school without my brother. He'll be at our old school sitting with his friends; my friends will pass by, or sometimes our groups will even combine, but I won't be there. I'll be alone in the new school in Marin.

There is no way he's abandoning me like this. I call him, but it goes directly to voice mail as I should have expected. There's no service at Dad's, which is why I sometimes feel stir crazy there. If it weren't still before six in the morning, I'd call the house, but I don't want to wake Dad and Tiffany.

Carson and I fight like cats and dogs; there's no way around that truth. But especially since the divorce, we end up doing a lot together. And though we don't hug and say, "I love you," or smile fondly at one another, we have a pretty close relationship—though neither of us would admit it too readily.

This is something I can't even imagine.

After our predawn breakfast, mostly in silence, Uncle Jimmy leaves, and the rest of us all eventually fall back to sleep. Aunt Jenna wakes me at ten to get ready for my first day of work.

I dial Dad's house, and he answers.

"Dad, what's going on with Carson? Is he there?"

"No, he's at school."

"What's this about him not moving down?"

"Well, your brother would miss Cottonwood. He's not really a big-city person."

I can't believe what I'm hearing. Did Dad convince my brother to stay in one short day?

"He only has one more year of high school, and he can work at the hardware store over the summer."

I glance at the clock. "Dad, I have to go, sorry. I'm starting work with Aunt Jenna today. I'll call back tonight. But tell Carson I called."

Dad says his usual endearing "Okay, good-bye, sweetie," and I rush for the bathroom.

Later, as I blow-dry my hair, my phone beeps. I expect it to be Carson, but the name surprises me.

NICK: Hey there Rubes, I'm sitting in Spanish II, Como estas?

ME: Bien. is that right? I took French. Bon. How are you?

NICK: Fine, but I missed your empty seat in alg last
period. So you haven't started school yet?

ME: Monday. I start work at my aunt's coffeehouse today.

NICK: Sounds cool. Maybe someday I'll show up there for
a coffee. How far away are you?

ME: Three to four hours.

This doesn't even sound like Nick. He's never this talkative.

NICK: Is it three or is it four?

ME: Depends on traffic.

NICK: I have a cousin at Berkeley. He wants me to come down. Are you near?

ME: Across the Bay, not too far. My stepdad thinks I should go to Berkeley for college.

NICK: Cool. Hey gotta go. Mr. Finkle keeps glancing my way. I think he's on to me.

ME: No problema. That's Spanish for no problem.

NICK: Thanks. I'll write later. Want to ask you something.

ME: Don't keep me in suspense.

NICK: Oh but I am.

ME: Meany

NICK: Yep. Crap, gotta run. Bye Marin girl.

ME: TTYL

"I think your mom will talk Carson into moving down," Aunt Jenna says as she drives faster than usual. We're late. The convertible top is up, and a thin fog covers the sky.

"He has Dad and all his friends up there. I think he likes Alexi Henders too."

I know my brother. And now I remember the many hesitations he had about moving down. I ignored them, thinking he'd adjust soon enough. Still, how could he drop a bomb like this without any warning—and over voice mail?

Aunt Jenna drives a narrow hilly back road that keeps us

from the traffic of Highway 101. "Guess we can't really blame him. He'll be a senior in the fall. Maybe if we found him a girl down here . . ."

I nod, but with little hope attached to it. The realization that I won't be with Carson during his senior year, that we won't live together—it's too staggering for me to fully process. I just can't think about it right now.

Aunt Jenna pulls into a parking place. I've been to the Underground Coffeehouse & Theater a few times. Baskets dripping with vines and flowers hang from the wooden eaves. Around the side is the opening to a courtyard where more shops and restaurants are tucked into the nooks and crannies of brick walkways with surprise flower beds and colored lights.

Aunt Jenna gets out quickly and carries in a bag of groceries. One of her employees has been here for several hours already. As we walk through the back door, my aunt transforms. It's not like a Jekyll/Hyde conversion, but she goes from fun and happy aunt to stressed and businesslike.

I scurry after her to the tiny office, where she plops down her jacket and purse.

"I'm warning you, this is the worst day to be your first day. I'm sorry for that. Usually we'd train you on a slower day. I'll give you a tour in a few minutes—just follow me around for now. I need to see how Rayna's surviving the morning crowd."

Aunt Jenna heads off after tossing me a black apron, which I tie around my waist. She's not usually neurotic, but when she dumps espresso beans into the grinder while introducing me to Rayna and assessing the needs, I'm worried her hand will soon be a finely ground blend.

Aunt Jenna talks over the grinding and, thankfully, pulls her hand from the machine. "We're already short-staffed. Terri forgot to put her India health trip on the calendar for this week, and without proper training on Premiere Night . . . oh, you'll just have to do what you can!"

And so here I am at the Underground. Aunt Betty was a silent partner until she gave Aunt Jenna the entire business after her marriage to Herbert. She said, "I want to see my nieces enjoying their inheritance before I die." Thus Mom got the house and Aunt Jenna the business. Carson and I wanted to ask about any early gifts to great-nephews and -nieces but decided against it.

On the street level, the Underground is a coffeehouse decorated in an Old World style. There are thick tables and chairs of different woods and shapes. Several tables have old theater chairs around them. I can imagine a Viennese coffeehouse when I'm here, except for the absence of cigarette smoke lingering in the air—I've read that's what it's like in a Viennese coffeehouse.

Downstairs are the cinema rooms with red velvet theater chairs, couches, dangling lights of all colors, and framed old-movie posters—some with autographs from the stars or directors. Two independent films play every week, and cinemagoers can take pastries, coffee, or a bag of Aunt Jenna's famous kettle corn varieties down to snack on during the movie.

Aunt Jenna explains all this as I follow her around the coffeehouse checking the cream and sugar, cleaning off tables, being introduced to customers.

"This is my wonderful niece, Ruby," Aunt Jenna says with her arm around my waist. It's when she speaks to customers that a calm friendliness returns and for a moment all the work and needs of the café are on hold.

"Isn't she a doll," an elderly lady exclaims.

"She most certainly is, and we'll have her running the coffee-house and the cinema before too long—this is a sharp one."

"Oh, she looks like it. And cute as a button as well."

I smile. Sometimes I imagine I'll be Aunt Jenna's partner someday, and we'll have a chain of Undergrounds in funky little towns up and down the California coast. Santa Cruz, Mendocino, Half Moon Bay, Carmel, Santa Barbara . . . But there are so many things I want to do . . .

When I follow her behind the counter, it's back-to-business Aunt Jenna.

"Let's get you familiar with the espresso machine. But during the busy times, I'll keep you on the cash register, since you have some experience from your dad's store."

"You know, I don't really know what Premiere Night is," I say as Aunt Jenna bends inside the display case to straighten the bakery items.

She's muttering something I can't hear, then pokes her head back out and calls toward the kitchen, "Rayna, are you finished with the quiche?"

Rayna peeks through the opening that separates the front counter from the kitchen. "Yep, it's cooling. But the cinnamon rolls aren't rising very well, and we need to buy some mushrooms and sun-dried tomatoes . . . and some brie."

"If we don't have time, I think we'll be okay. The popcorn is most important."

Aunt Jenna turns to me as I stand awkwardly behind her,

knowing she needs help, but what do I do? My dad's hardware store is a lot different from a coffeehouse. There I mostly sat on a stool and watched. Sometimes I worked the cash register or rode around with him on the forklift.

And I still don't know what Premiere Night is.

"We're becoming quite known for our gourmet popcorn. This month's special is White Chocolate Cinnamon—and then we have our normal buttered popcorn; plain caramel or Caramel Supreme with cashews, almonds, and pecans; and Choco Supreme."

"Yum. I better sample it all," I say with a smile. "Will I learn to make it?"

"Yes, but not today. Rayna will be in the kitchen until she leaves at four o'clock. I'm hoping to get your mom or a friend to come relieve you at six—oh, I forgot to get the butter out of the freezer—oh, we need to . . ."

Her words turn to muttering again, and I stand behind the counter gazing around. "What can I do?"

Aunt Jenna stops as her eyes move around the room. "Uh, uh . . . wash all the tables, refill the sugars—we use both natural sugar and refined . . . whatever you see that needs doing. Then I'll teach you the espresso machine and juicer, and if you could make sure all the theater rooms are clean—they should be, but you never know. Somewhere around here we have a list that explains our drinks . . . We have three hours before the hordes arrive."

"For Premiere Night," I say, hoping this reminds her to answer my question.

"No, for the after-school rush." My aunt stops her frenzied movements and smiles. "I'm sorry, Ruby Red, it's a crazy day.

32

Premiere Night. You see, every week we show two independent films in the theaters downstairs. But every three months we have amateur night for local filmmakers—a lot of them are from the college and high school. They get to premiere their latest shorts— short films."

"Ah," I say with a smile. "So we're about to be inundated with a horde of artsy, filmmaking, high school and college-aged guys—good-looking too, I hope?"

My aunt laughs. "Yes, some are. Now let's get to work. Good service is why my customers keep returning—that and the awesome gourmet popcorn, which I need to start making, and the movies, and the coffee . . ." She winks at me.

I clean the tables as a few people enter and place their orders. Aunt Jenna, despite her anxiety, is amazing in her ability to appear calm and lively around the customers. She's witty and friendly while her hands move around the espresso contraption.

Sometimes I find it interesting to think of all the hundreds and thousands of people who are walking into a coffee shop somewhere in the world right at this exact moment. Taste buds yearning, the milk steaming, the conversations in nearly every language on earth. I picture an old Turkish man with a tiny steaming cup of strong espresso or . . .

"Ruby." Rayna interrupts my daydreaming.

"Yes?" I return to earth and set a dirty plate and cup in the kitchen sink.

"While I have a few minutes, why don't I show you the espresso machine?"

"Sure."

Sounds easy enough . . . but Rayna's instructions sound like

Open this, dump this here, get this, put this here and that here, press that, wait for this, and that's a shot of espresso.

I know she uses more precise words, but that's how it comes to me before she says, "Oh, I forgot the butter was on the stove. Hope that helps. Why don't you experiment for a bit until your aunt can show you more."

I open the thingie where you put the espresso, and a splash of watery grounds shoots all over my apron. At least the apron's black. I think I'm figuring it out, but when I push the button, water comes out in the other spot, and then I overflow the soy milk when I try steaming it. I step away from the espresso machine and decide to search for more dirty dishes and tables. The dining area has many nooks and crannies between tall plants, half walls, and wooden cabinets with pottery for sale.

And then a cute guy walks through the door.

"Hey there, Frankie, you're out early," Aunt Jenna calls with a smile.

He rubs his eyes. "I'm actually out late. Was up all night working. I get special home credit when I'm working on film projects."

"I thought you were going to enforce deadlines on your group—no finishing the night before."

"Yeah, I talk big. Hey, I'm dropping off the programs. And since I'm here, I'll get my usual."

"You can be Ruby's first victim. This is my niece, Ruby. Ruby, this is one of my very favorite customers, Frankie Klarken."

"Nice to meet you," we both say.

"So where have you been hiding her?" Frankie asks.

"She's from up north. Near Redding."

34

Frankie sets a handful of brochures on the counter, then leans on his elbows. "Redding? I'm unaware of California outside the Bay. Even LA is lost directionally to me. I think it might be that way . . ." And he spins his finger from west to north to east.

"Frankie always gets a German Chocolate Blended with two add-shots."

"Uh, okay," I say. "So—"

"I'll start the espresso," Aunt Jenna says. "And you put three pumps of the organic chocolate into one of the large cups."

I try following my aunt's instructions while Frankie watches from the counter. He leans forward, his light brown hair dipping over one eye. He appears amused by our performance.

"Wow, girls, you've really got the flow of teamwork there," he says and laughs loudly after I spill the ground espresso over Aunt Jenna's apron.

There's something that whispers into my mind about Frankie even as I'm completely stressed about making his drink. I ignore it for now and try listing out the process, determined not to continue making this a disaster:

1. *Dump old espresso from (thing)—bang it until clean.*
2. *Grind beans.*
3. *Fill (thing), attach, twist.*
4. *Hit button for one or two shots.* I do this twice, since Frankie wants a total of four shots of espresso in his drink.
5. *Oh yeah, don't forget to put the shot glass under the release.* I redo one of the shots.
6. *Milk, soy, or rice milk*—Frankie wants milk. "Not the skim kind, baby face." *Do I have a baby face?* I wonder.

7. *Steam milk until thermometer reaches at least 180 degrees.*
8. *Add shots of flavor if needed.* For the German Chocolate Blended, we use a shot and a half of coconut syrup and a half shot of hazelnut, which I pour into the shot glasses.
9. *Add three pumps of chocolate*—then one more because Frankie says, "I like my chocolate, can't have enough of the chocolate."
10. *For blended, we put the espresso shots, milk, flavored syrups, and chocolate in the blender with ice. Blend, pour, top with whipped cream and more chocolate syrup.* Done.

"Okay, there you go," I say, handing him the drink.

Aunt Jenna and I wait as he takes the smallest perceptible sip. He makes a slight grimace before the smile. "Mmm."

"If you don't like it, we'll redo it," I say. "I did wonder if I grabbed the sugar-free coconut."

"No, girl, it's just a little different."

"Different?"

"Different doesn't mean bad, now, does it? Look at me—I'm different. Is that a bad thing? But I'd better run. Much to do before tonight." He says this as he's leaving, calling at the door, "See you tonight. Nice to meet you, Ruby, and thanks."

My aunt and I stare after him a moment, until I finally say, "He didn't like it, did he?"

Aunt Jenna does that little scrunchy face she gets when trying to tell me something without hurting my feelings. "It's not that he didn't like it."

"He hated it."

"Yeah, he hated it."

"And he's gay?"

My aunt nods her head. "Yep."

"Bummer."

We stare at the door after Frankie, look at each other, and laugh. But then the door opens and the horde arrives.

chapter five

"Please, no more coffee," I protest with my hands up in surrender.

After my preliminary espresso disaster, Aunt Jenny asked me to watch every espresso drink she made for the next hour while I worked the register. Her hands moved fast, and I asked her to slow down a few times.

Then the samples began. She wanted me to distinguish between a cappuccino, latte, café mocha—how soy and rice milk changed the flavor, not to mention the different add-shots that include every flavor you can imagine. I spotted a "cheesecake" (interesting) and even a "blood orange" (ick!). In the sampling, I discovered some new coffee favorites like almond biscotti latte and Mexican café mocha. But enough is enough.

Aunt Jenna pushes the little cup toward me. "Okay, but this one is s'more. It's a mocha with marshmallow and graham cracker flavorings."

I give her a sickened look—this has to be my twentieth sample.

"But are you getting an idea of the different flavors and intensities?"

"Am I ever." I may become a tea person after this espresso overdose.

"Good," she says with a laugh. "Now take a break before we get ready for the filmies. You can go around the corner for gourmet pizza, or there's a great salad place on the next block."

I take off my apron in the small back room and search for my phone to tell Kate about the cute gay guy I met and my new favorite coffee drinks. My phone is nowhere to be found in the holes and pockets of my bag. I dump out everything—my wallet, photos, gum wrappers, notes from friends, pens and pencils. Then I remember: it's sitting at home charging in the window of my bedroom. Oh bother.

My hands shake from the caffeine, and my stomach longs for something to combat the sweets, so I'm off to a late lunch somewhere. But self-consciousness pervades me as I walk toward the outside door. People have come in and out of the Underground for the last four hours, going about their business. I find it strangely hard to force myself out the front doors. I even consider getting a scone and eating it in the back room.

Okay, Ruby, you're fifteen years old. You can walk down the street, do a little window shopping, buy some lunch.

"Can I get you anything?" I ask the one couple in the room, who basically ignore me as they lean in and talk in romantic tones.

The tables are nearly empty now, but I feel vaguely guilty to be on lunch while Aunt Jenna clears them. "Do you want me to stay and help?"

"No, no, go explore a bit. The fog burned off, and it's a beautiful day. If you find Greens, get me an Asian salad with dressing on the side. Do you need money?"

"Mom gave me some."

One last glance around the safety of the coffeehouse, and I push myself into the warm sunlight of midafternoon. These brick grottos are full of interesting shops and boutiques. I notice a handcraft toy shop that Kate would love to explore with me, and a shop with musical instruments from all over the world dangling from the ceiling and resting against the wide windows.

But I don't find Greens because the farthest I venture is to the gourmet pizza parlor in the courtyard next door. I reach for my cell phone to call Aunt Jenna about getting a pizza instead. Argh! No cell phone . . .

Without my cell, I'm truly alone. It feels like going to the mall and realizing I've forgotten my shoes. As I get in line at the counter, I hear someone else's phone beep, and I look around like a hungry orphan at a banquet.

The walls of Antonio's Gourmet Pizza are covered in pictures of famous people standing beside the owner, presumably Antonio. Harrison Ford, Cameron Diaz, Tom Hanks, the lead singer of Green Day, and others I recognize but whose names I don't know.

The counter girl asks me if I want the couscous crust, and I say yes simply because I don't know what it is. I sigh when I walk away, tired of feeling stupid. The tables are full, but I see a guy leave a table outside. That's where I sit, with the number 17 on the iron tabletop.

The day is blue and bright. Hanging baskets cascade flowers from light poles along the street, and I think what a beautiful town this is. When have I done something like go to a restaurant alone? Never, I realize. I haven't done anything alone in my fifteen years that I can think of. Even when I'm alone in my room, I have connections all around, thanks to the miracle of technology. Me at this wrought-iron table beside a huge planter of red geraniums waiting for my couscous pizza with people all around me—this is alone.

So this is what it'd be like in Europe, sitting at an outdoor café with the French or the Swedes (is it too cold in Sweden for outdoor cafés?) or the Austrians or . . . whatever country I'm in. Could I do it alone? Mom says that all the truest journeys are done alone, even if traveling with companions. It's the inner journey that matters.

And strangely, just sitting here at a little table in this corner café, I sense such a journey stretching out before me. Once my pizza arrives, I lean back in the chair, cross my legs, and drink a sparkling mineral water.

But okay, when a lady's phone beeps, I do reach for my purse.

When I get back to the Underground, the clock says 3:15. Kate and everyone will be out of school. Maybe she's at track practice. Carson will be hanging out with his friends. Little Tony's family will probably be making funeral arrangements, picking out his clothing, buying a coffin and plot of ground for his grave.

I try shoving those terrible thoughts out of my head, and instead I wonder if Nick will ask me to the upcoming prom. After all, he finally knows he likes me, and he wants to ask me something. There's a dress in a store window down the street. I caught a glimpse of it on the drive in. It's lime green and black, with a skirt that would twirl if I felt like twirling.

I imagine all kinds of *Sound of Music* twirling as I work in the coffeehouse. I imagine that I glance up at one of the customers and there's Nick. His arrival is like the scene in *Chocolat* when Johnny Depp returns to the little chocolaterie for Juliette Binoche. Who couldn't feel that all the way through the toes? What happens next as the movie credits roll . . . who knows and who cares? We know he's taking her from her loneliness, and they'll love each other for the rest of their lives.

"Ruby!" Aunt Jenna says loudly, making me jump and realize she's been calling my name for a while. "Off in Rubyland again?"

"Sorry."

"One of our regulars, Natasha, is at her table by the corner window. She's waiting for a ginger currant scone and chai tea with rice milk. The tea is on the counter—just pour some rice milk from the lower fridge into a cream server."

Natasha isn't easy to locate. I hadn't noticed the tiny table tucked behind the indoor stone fountain in a corner by the window. She's fully engrossed in a book with a stack of other books and sketches spread out on the small table, making it impossible for me to set down the tea saucer and plate.

"Excuse me," I say in a library-soft voice—why, I'm not sure.

She looks up as if surprised to see me, as if surprised to find herself sitting at her usual spot in my aunt's café/movie house. It's not a ditzy sort of look, but one that makes me think she's still somewhere else, in whatever place that book took her.

"Oh yes, I apologize. Let me make some room."

She's old—like maybe fifty—and beautiful. I think she's the most beautiful older woman I've met. Her hair is cut short, very short, in a way only certain women can pull off—and she's one of those certain women for sure. Her earrings are black pearls, and she wears a matching black pearl necklace.

"What are you reading?" I ask.

"Short stories from a Croatian writer," she says, turning the book over. She moves her books to a chair and thanks me as I set her tea and scone beside a paper with notes scribbled on it.

"Croatia? Is that in Europe?"

"Former Yugoslavia—Eastern Europe. Croatia is next on my list of places to visit—the Dalmatian Coast, to be precise. I'm hoping to go in the autumn, and then I'll head for my favorite place to visit in October—the Austrian Alps. Have you ever been to Europe?"

I smile. "Uh, no. I haven't. Not yet."

"That's the spirit. I believe you most certainly will, and not too far in the future." Natasha gives me a confident look, as if she can see it clearly.

I can't talk any longer; we have a large order for a team of advertisers having a board meeting.

As I'm cleaning tables later, I imagine myself over at Natasha's table in thirty or more years. I'm chatting with a teenaged girl, telling her how I once worked here and then all about my world travels, encouraging her to venture out as well. The girl might ask about the book I'm reading. An art book written by me, or a travel guide written by me, or maybe it's written by someone else, but I'm planning my next trip. My handsome husband shows up—Nick?—who says he's booked our tickets and we'll be spending the summer on a lake in Italy or on the coast of Brazil or in a small beach hut in the Cook Islands.

"Ruby," Aunt Jenna calls, and again I realize that she's called me more than once.

I really need to control my daydreaming.

My shift should be over. No one can give me a ride home. If Carson were here . . . but he isn't, I remind myself. And he won't be. I suppose I'll need to learn public transportation. There's no such thing in Cottonwood, unless you count hopping on the nearest horse you see in a field.

I overhear Aunt Jenna on the phone, panic in her tone. "How sick are you? I know you're sorry, but I just don't know what I'm going to do tonight." She hangs up and is punching in more numbers.

"I thought you left," she says as I come into the kitchen.

"No ride. Austin can get me in an hour, but I can stay and help."

"Where's your mom?"

"She's interviewing the owner of that boutique for one of her magazines."

"What boutique?" But Aunt Jenna is by now flipping pages on her board, looking for any help.

"Listen, it's no problem, Aunt Jenna. It's not like I have plans."

She sighs. "I will make this up to you."

"That sounds good," I say with a smile. "Let me just make a phone call, and I'll be back out there."

Ruby Unscripted

Aunt Jenna nods; then she closes her eyes, takes a deep breath, and leaves with a renewed cheery look on her face. "Premiere Night officially begins."

The only thing that made me hesitate about volunteering for tonight was my phone. My poor lonely phone, sitting on the windowsill in my room, ringing inconsolably with no one to comfort it. And what's been happening back home? My friends will think I've died. Nick might be annoyed that I'm not around for whatever he needs to ask me. Prom, prom?

Mac answers the phone at the house.

"Hey, it's Ruby. I need you to do me a favor."

"Okay, but it's gonna cost you."

"Cost me? Cost me what?"

"Dearly."

"Huh?"

"I saw that on a movie. They said, 'It's gonna cost you dearly.' What's a dearly?"

"Listen, I can't talk long."

"So you don't know either?"

"I'll explain later."

"So you do know? Just tell me."

"Mac! Listen to me. I need you to go up to my phone in my room and send Kate a text message."

"Oh yeah, your phone keeps vibrating. I put one of my army men on it, and he stayed on for three seconds."

"Mac. Focus. Listen to me. Get my phone."

"Okay, hang on. It was plugged in over here . . ."

"You're in my room?"

"Mom and Austin are putting up my bunk beds, so they said

45

I could play in here. Where'd your phone go? I built a Lego fortress around it—oh, here it is!"

"Great. Now do you remember how to send a text?"

"It says you have twenty new messages."

I hear a few beeps.

"And six missed calls."

"Missed calls?" That could mean something. My friends only call when something's important.

"Do you want me to read your messages to you?"

"No! Just go to contacts—do you see the button you push beneath contacts? Then scroll down, you'll see the arrow keys—"

"I play games on Mom's phone, remember. I know how it works."

"Okay, send a text to Kate. Just say Ruby is at work and forgot her phone at home. She'll call when she's back."

"I better write that down."

My aunt calls my name from the front counter.

"I have to go—just remember it. You're just telling her I don't have my phone, and I'll call when I'm home from work."

"Home from work, will call . . ."

I hear people in the dining area of the coffeehouse.

"Promise you'll put my phone back after that."

"It's gonna cost you."

"Dearly, yes, I know."

He laughs at that.

"I could take messages for you. 'Ruby's phone, Mac speaking.' See how good I'd be."

"No. Just send that to Kate and nothing else."

"Oops."

The last thing you want to hear your ten-year-old brother say when he's using your phone is "Oops."

"What happened?"

"I might have erased your messages."

"What?!"

"I didn't mean to."

"Ruby," Aunt Jenna calls again.

"Okay, forget it. Just leave my phone alone."

"Sorry."

"Mac"—I want to yell a slew of things at him right now—"now you owe me for this one."

"Yeah. I owe you dearly."

chapter six

Kate, it's so cool, I wish you were here.

This is what I *want* to type, if I had my phone with me.

I miss Kate terribly, wish I had her beside me, helping customers and whispering comments about the people who've come for Premiere Night.

The air simply buzzes with excitement like static electricity in your clothing.

"Ruby, take over the cash register—I need to make another batch of popcorn," Aunt Jenna says. I see the tiredness in her eyes, but we have several hours yet to go.

Premiere Night brings out a different crowd from the daytime customers. Or maybe it's some of the same people, but the night and event have transformed them into cool creatures of the art and film world. Artists wear their baggy jeans and expensive but faded T-shirts, a few visible tattoos, piercings, gauges in their ears, while other artist-types express wealth in their clothes, watches, and jewelry. Several of the girls look like runway models, and a few others could've been extras at the sorority house in *Legally Blonde*. My dirty black apron, Gap jeans, brown shoes, and Underground polo shirt don't mix with any of the types here. And I can only guess what my hair and makeup look like, since I've been here since eleven in the morning.

I see Frankie. He waves and winks at me from a circle of people who talk and move like a flock of birds through the coffeehouse and down the stairs.

Kate would love this, and all the very hot guys. We're always complaining about the lack of good-looking males at home, though I think that's because we've known most of the guys at school since they were eating paste and pulling our ponytails. But if she were here, we could take up my aunt and mom's hobby of creating stories for the most interesting characters. We might say that the guy with the Mohawk works at a tattoo parlor but has a secret love for poodles. The twin girls near the corner who look shy and unpretentious are daughters of a senator and plot to take the most-famous-twins throne from the Olsen sisters.

I miss Kate. I miss her with a strange gut-ache feeling. Or maybe it's a mixture of loneliness and missing.

A dark-haired guy weaves through the groupings of people. His eyes—dark brown and serious—catch mine for a moment, then he walks toward the cinema stairs. Maybe it's his intensity or a way about his casual style that reminds me of a young Johnny Depp. There's also a young Brad Pitt and Tom Cruise and surely Chad Michael Murray's younger brother.

The upstairs crowd soon disappears into the cinemas downstairs. I carry a few more empty mugs to the kitchen, where Aunt

Jenna comes out of the walk-in cooler carrying an armload of containers. "Oh, Ruby, you should go see some of the films."

But there are dirty tables to wipe, and popcorn litters the floor, and Aunt Jenna looks increasingly tired, which makes me worry. She's had health issues for a number of years, which is also why she hasn't had a baby.

Uncle Jimmy arrived some time ago and is doing dishes, though ever so slowly compared to Rayna. He keeps having trouble with the industrial dishwasher. He's still in his jeans and T-shirt from being on a building site where he's the foreman of a construction company.

"Next time," I say and return to the dining area.

From the stairwell I hear shouts and applause rising from the theater below. I overhear snippets of conversation as people come up and down for coffee, popcorn, and sweets. The monthly special of popcorn runs out, and Aunt Jenna gives up trying to make more.

"We're in survival mode now," she says.

I take in the conversations . . . a wallflower no one really notices. It's an illuminating position. I get to overhear a lot.

"That was the best I've seen."

"We've got this night bagged, there's no doubt. That film was perfect."

"Let's go to the beach after this."

"Sure. Tell everyone to meet at the cove by Shellee's."

"Who is that with Shellee?"

"I don't know, but he was staring at Blair, or so she said."

"Blair thinks everyone's staring at her. Okay, they probably are."

"I don't think she's as great as everyone makes her out to be."

"Are Crystal and Dylan still broken up? I saw her in his car this afternoon."

They are the conversations of teenagers anywhere. These live in a different place, the names aren't the same, and they have different interests from the kids back home, but overall the themes and emotions are the same. Socialize, make plans, dream big, have fun. The chemistry and angst between guys and girls, friendships and loves.

The conversations make me miss home. Remind me of people who know me, who talk about me for the good and the bad, who want to hang out with me. They're all far away right now.

Will some of these people become my friends? I search their faces, looking for some telltale sign. Sometimes I've imagined going back in time to see myself walking by a future friend in the mall or at school. Maybe as a little kid, one of my future best friends played on the same playground as me. I wonder if I've walked past my future husband, if the love of my life might be in the cinema downstairs, or if he's driving some highway with the music loud and an ache of longing in his chest for the mysterious *her* who is me, and only me.

Another group lingers near the counter, and I catch bits of conversations.

"Hey, did you ask your parents if we'll meet them in Barcelona or Marseilles this summer?"

"They haven't figured out the plan yet. My dad's in Germany ordering a new Porsche. He couldn't wait to see it, so he flew over to check out the production."

"Oh, did you hear that Jeff is interning on a Francis Ford Coppola film this summer?"

I smile at that. Okay, so not all teen conversations are the same everywhere. And these may not be my future friends after all.

Picking up a few empty cups, I turn toward the counter and see the dark-haired Johnny Depp guy coming from the kitchen. Customers aren't supposed to be there, but he acts as if he works here. For all I know, he might. We pass each other with a quick glance.

Aunt Jenna is washing dishes when I bring a tray back, and Uncle Jimmy is doing something with tools under the sink.

"The coffeehouse is officially closed," she says. "They'll clear out within the hour, but no more serving anything. You could run down and see what's happening in the theater."

I shake my head. "I'll finish cleaning up in the dining area."

"Feeling awkward with the other kids your age?" Uncle Jimmy teases, poking his head out from beneath the sink.

"Who, me?" I say with a smile.

Aunt Jenna gives me a sympathetic sigh. "Oh, sweetie, it'll become home soon enough. You won't feel displaced for long."

"Uh-huh," I say, trying to sound as though I believe her, knowing she's probably right. "The people here really are mostly rich, much richer than at home. And they're making films and going to Barcelona for summer vacation instead of playing mini golf and laser tag and going to the lake."

"I'm sure they do those things too. And you didn't really fit in with the mini golf and lake crowd anyway. Believe me, it took some adjusting for me too. You aren't the only one who grew up in little Cottonwood."

I grab the broom from a hook and ask, "What made it hard for you?"

"Well, I'm the only woman in my Bible study who works because she really has to. One woman complains about her job as an interior designer. She says she wishes she could quit, but they just can't afford it. She drives a Beemer and has a rock on her hand the size of an Easter egg. The concept of money is very different.

"And then there are the vacations and the education. I know a homemaker with a PhD, and most of the others have a master's. I didn't finish college. But if you have a strong sense of who you are, what you believe, and God's purpose for you, you'll have no trouble with anyone you meet your entire life." Aunt Jenna glances up at the wall clock. "Oh, wow, you've been here twelve hours."

"Both of us have been here twelve hours."

"I'll have to do something to pay you back. Oh, and I totally forgot—he was just here too!"

"What? Who was here?"

"I meant to introduce you to Kaden."

"Kaden, the yard and moving boy again?" I ask.

Uncle Jimmy looks up again. "He tried helping with the dishwasher problem, but I sent him to focus on his film."

Aunt Jenna interjects, like they're a team selling a car. "He did a short film last year that won some contest and gained critical acclaim. He's involved with media at a church I want your mom and Austin to try out. I guarantee you'll think he's hot the moment you see him. But I think he was leaving—we should try to catch him."

It's always funny to me when Aunt Jenna says things like "You'll think he's hot."

But then suddenly I think of the guy I saw coming out of the kitchen. The one with the dark eyes and serious expression.

"What does this Kaden look like?"

It's nearly midnight before we get back to the house. It feels like the week I went to Mexico with the youth mission trip. Well, actually, it's not like that at all, except for how long it feels since I've been home, since I've talked to my friends. My head is spinning from exhaustion, but I have to see who wrote me.

My phone sits on the windowsill, partly plugged into the wall. Beneath it is a white sheet of paper that says, "Ruby, I am very very sorry I messed up your texts. I cleaned your room and made you a snack. Love, Mac."

There's a plate of Wheat Thins with orange cheese melted on top, and even though it's hours old, I try one. Not bad.

Even with what Mac deleted, I have fifteen new texts. From Kate, Isabelle, Randy, Felicity, and Nikki. And to think I felt alone today. But I am surprised to find nothing from Nick or Carson. Maybe those were ones that Mac erased.

KATE: What was that half message you sent Jake about
    forgetting your phone.
KATE: Hello??!
KATE: Should I call for search and rescue?
KATE: You MUST call me ASAP!
ISABELLE: I hate Nikki. How could she think what she did
    would be okay?

RANDY: Now that you're gone, I might as well tell you
     that I was the one who sent you the rose-a-gram
     last year on Valentine's. But don't tell Angie. She
     always thought I had a thing for you and now that
     we're going out . . .

I decide to read the rest of that bizarre text later.

FELICITY: Josh asked me to the dance. You always give me
     the best advice. What should I do? Josh is really
     cute, but you know how I feel about Harlen . . .

I skip this one too and move on.

NIKKI: Hey girl. How's the big city? So I need to know. Do
     you like Nick or what? I'll back off if you do, you
     know I will. Everyone says you've got this great new
     life down there so I didn't think you'd mind that I
     asked him to prom. Tell me if you do.
NIKKI: Uh-oh. Kate said you'd want to go to prom with
     Nick, that you'd come home for it. I suck! I can tell
     him that you want to go with him instead. He said
     yes when I asked. I know it's pretty bold of a girl,
     but I thought why not?

I've been gone a few days, Nick finally likes me, but now he's
going to the prom with Nikki? So is that au revoir to the lime
green dress with the twirly skirt?

55

chapter seven

Have I ever been this tired?

I've hardly slept the last few nights, and after working over twelve hours, the last thing I want is to get up at eight for a counseling appointment at my new school. But that's exactly what I'm doing.

My friends are all in class—Carson too—and most of my morning responses to last night have consisted of: Sorry, I left my phone at home, but I can't talk now. I have nothing to wear. I'm late already.

And to Isabelle: I don't even know what to say about Nikki.

And to Randy: Thanks for the rose-a-gram. I won't tell.

Before sending them, I deleted the words I wrote to Nikki. Silly junior high things like: Nick likes me now. Nick was supposed to ask me to the dance.

And to Nick I wrote: Hey, how's Spanish today? I have another day off from school. Jealous?

That isn't what I wanted to write, but my dad always says

don't burn your bridges unless you like swimming in freezing cold water with river eels, so I decide to wait till after my counseling appointment to decide what to say to that wimp, jerk . . .

"Wow," Mom says as we pull into the parking lot, and as I see the view before me, my mouth literally drops open.

The landscaped walkways and smooth stucco buildings with tall palm trees wave a welcome to us. Or they may be laughing at us, saying, "Who do you think you are to come here? This isn't for people like you."

"Are you sure this is the high school and not a university?" I ask.

"It's like no high school I've ever seen," Mom says in a tone that sounds nervous for me.

And then we notice the cars.

In Cottonwood you'd see every variety, from clunkers, minivans, and work trucks to sports cars. But here the student parking lot looks like a new car dealership. The glimmer of perfectly waxed paint is probably visible to orbiting satellites. When I get out of our Honda Accord (unwashed and with boxes in the backseat), I'm beside a silver BMW that I spontaneously want to put handprints all over.

We're going to my counselor's appointment, the one that Carson and I would have attended without our mommy in tow. But with Carson gone, I'll put aside my pride. I want my mommy with me.

At least I'm never embarrassed by my mom like some kids are. She's smart, pretty, confident, and young compared to a lot of mothers. She could pass for an older sister, almost.

The students, thankfully, are in class, except for one or two.

"You look nice," Mom says, which makes me even more self-conscious.

Is she saying that because I *don't* look nice? Because she thinks I need a boost to the ego, since I'm the third-class citizen here? I'd be in the lower deck of the *Titanic*. The ones who weren't given a life raft or vest . . .

"I see the office," Mom says, bringing me back from the icy waters of the North Sea.

I tell myself that there is no one better than me, that I will be myself and no one else, and a bunch of other stuff that just runs together in my head and keeps my feet going forward.

We find the office and secretary and sit down to await the counselor. There is a smallness about me. My clothes feel itchy and uncomfortable, and I wonder how my hair looks and if any dark hairs have frizzed out of my sleek ponytail.

A few people glance at me curiously as they pass, and I want to say, as Mac might, "Take a picture!"

Mr. James, my school counselor, greets us enthusiastically and ushers us into his office. His walls are covered with certificates, diplomas, awards, and photographs. He has stacks of catalogs from colleges and papers in unorganized piles on his desk around his flat-screen computer monitor.

"And your son, will he be coming?"

Mom shakes her head and doesn't hide her disappointment as she says, "No, he'll be remaining at his school in Cottonwood."

Carson and Mom talked last night while I was at the Underground. He feels bad, Mom said, but he still wants to stay with Dad. He's going to hear about it from me, that's for sure.

The counselor nods with a sympathetic knowing look that's more annoying than anything else.

After having us sit, Mr. James talks. And boy, can he talk. Mom and I glance at each other about three minutes into it.

"Oh, you'll really enjoy our school. I've been here two years now, and it's the best school I've worked at. We have excellent programs, excellent opportunities, a student body that excels in academics, art, athletics, and even politics. According to your file, you're a moderately academic student, Ruby, though your state test scores are impressive and your teacher comments are very complimentary."

Ever since I was in sixth grade, teachers have talked about pushing us. "This year will not be easy—it's to prepare you for high school . . . The college prep classes will get you ready for college . . ." Everything is about preparing for something in the future. For college, for your job, for your kids, for your retirement, for your death. When does anyone get to enjoy the moment?

I like enjoying the moment. And my grades sometimes reflect that, much to the consternation of Mom and my teachers. Dad doesn't care so much, as long as I pass.

"Yes, if she applied herself, she'd have a high grade point average. We've had a rough few years—" Mom sees my look that says, *Please don't bring up the divorce again.* And then says, "So, uh, I think this change will be a great opportunity for her."

"Oh, it will indeed, indeed. I see that you take a lot of art courses, Miss Madden."

"Yes."

"Let's see what we can find that interests you. I believe a

happy student is one who excels. We have 450 sophomores, and over 80 percent are involved in some club or activity."

"Four hundred fifty?"

"And our cafeteria isn't like most schools. We offer home-made soups, locally grown organic vegetables, whole grains for the breads and pizza dough. Everything is as natural and healthy as possible. Our programs are . . ."

My mind sort of zones out as I imagine describing all of this to Kate and my friends back home, telling how Mr. James turns red in his excited description of the high school.

"I love this school," Mr. James says. "We've had a few movies shot on the school grounds as well."

This interests me, until he starts naming movies that are long before my time, a few even before Mom's, and then a bunch of short indie films that no normal person would know.

"Cool," I say.

"That's interesting. I'll have to put those on my iMovie list." Mom is ever so polite.

I unzip my purse and search for my phone. Even though I keep telling myself to put it in the little interior pocket, I never do, and I have to dig around the bottom to find it. There it is. I view it inside my purse and see a new message from Kate.

You r not going to believe this!

I think this is Kate's new replacement for "Hello."

I talked to Meg who has chem with Nick. She said Nick told her . . .

Mom nudges me with her elbow and frowns.

The words *Nikki* and *prom* are the last ones I see before dropping the phone back into my purse.

Mr. James is still talking. "Look for the daily bulletin . . . sports teams . . . AP and honors classes . . . What are some of your other interests, Ruby?"

Questions always bring me back to focus. "Um, well . . ." My mind is blank. Strangely blank. Mine. I'm usually so full of ideas and interests and things I want to pursue that I can't pick one.

But right now, while sitting in the school that feels as foreign as one in Japan, I can't think of anything I want to do, except go home to Cottonwood and have my normal life back. I'm interested in that. I'm interested in what dress I'd wear to prom if Nick dumped Nikki, and interested in whether he'd like lime green and black—he could get a lime green shirt with black tie, or would it look better the opposite? Yes, the opposite. I really want that lime green dress at that dress shop near the Underground. On the drive home, I saw it again with a light shining down like a promise of dances to come.

Mom says, "She likes different kinds of arts. And foreign languages. She wanted to take several classes that aren't offered anymore at her old school."

"That's happening more and more in small, rural communities. But not here. We have a lot to offer in our arts programs. And you'll be surprised at the variety of languages. We certainly have French. We even offer Mandarin."

"Mandarin?" *What would I do with Chinese?* I wonder, though maybe I'll tell Kate I'm taking that since she teases me so often about my ever-fluctuating interests.

We set up my schedule, and I pick French 1 and International Cooking for my electives.

Then Mr. James asks, "Do you know anyone who attends here?"

"I met a guy . . . Frankie something, maybe Clark, or Conklin?"

"Oh yes, Franklin Klarken is a wonderful young man. He's a little overly enthusiastic at times, and unfocused in his studies . . . but what a character. He's a junior this year, I believe. I try to know all of the students by name, but that goal keeps me on my toes. Anyway, I assigned a member of student council to show you around on Monday. She will be stopping by to meet you any minute now." He looks at a Marin High clock on the wall.

Mr. James and my mom talk away about the school programs and college opportunities while he types in my new schedule. A strange sort of panic washes over me, like a wave of sadness or fear or hysteria—maybe all three. My feet want to run from this place.

"Hi, Mr. James." A pretty face peeks into the room. Short brown hair and brown eyes. She's one of those natural beauties and wears only a subtle hint of makeup.

Mr. James stands up eagerly. "Come in, come in. Lucinda is the sophomore class treasurer, the head of debate club, and a track-and-field star."

"Wow," I say.

Lucinda motions like she's brushing away the compliment. "And I still won't get into Princeton unless I get my act together."

While Mom finishes with Mr. James, I follow Lucinda outside. She's my first real hope for useful information. And she might offer my first possibility of friendship.

"So where are you from again?"

"Near Redding. It's about three or four hours north."

She rests a knee on a bench the way a jock might, but she's so pretty it's sort of a humorous stance. "I've been as far north as Mendocino or Napa. Are there any spas up there?"

"Spas?"

"My mother is doing this tour of spas. She's in Budapest right now, but I know she's gone around California. She has this book about the best spas in the world and wants to try every one of them. I guess everyone needs goals."

I laugh. "Yeah, I guess so."

"I'm more like my father. I'd rather tour all the golf courses or the top architectural wonders."

"We're not really known for any of those things, though we have them. Like the Sundial Bridge, which is really cool. And Redding does have a church designed by Frank Lloyd Wright, but I suppose with all you have down here, that wouldn't be all that exciting."

"Yeah, probably not." The way she says that sounds just a touch snobbish, and I hope she doesn't mean it.

"So you're in student government?"

"Yes. Both of my parents were in student gov at this school. My dad is thinking of running for Congress next term. He's so political, but international bankers make much more money than government officials, so he has his strategy. I've been very *encouraged* to do politics, to the point of insistent encouragement. But I actually enjoy it. I'm considering political science for my major in college."

"Interesting."

Lucinda waves as some students pass and gives a smile that I think will get her definite votes.

"I'm supposed to ask what some of your interests are to help you find some groups or organizations. You know, get you plugged into the school quickly."

"I'm about as political as a . . . well, what's the most non-political thing in existence?"

"Everyone is political, whether they admit it or not. But it's a rare person who is actually politician material," she says with a tinge of condescension.

"I like art."

"We have lots of art classes and art theory and art club. There's also yearbook staff, the newspaper, and dozens of clubs, from the Che Guevara group to Vegans Today . . . but I don't imagine you'd be interested in a lot of those. Are you interested in filmmaking? That's a big thing here."

"Well, yeah, maybe. I think some of the students hold a Premiere Night at my aunt's coffeehouse. I just started working there. The Underground—do you know it?"

"Ah sure, cool place. Did you say you *work* there?"

"Yeah."

Lucinda doesn't respond to that, just files it away with political smoothness. At home, most older teenagers have part-time jobs, but I wonder what it's like here where money is less of an issue.

"I'll introduce you to some of the filmies."

"Thanks."

"Okay, so you'll be here Monday?"

"Yep."

"Then I'll meet you right here at eight o'clock."

"Great."

"Off to my debate club." She smiles warmly and squeezes my arm. "You'll like it here, Ruby. I'll make sure you do."

"Thanks, Lucinda."

"If you need anything, call me at this number." She hands me a small CD thingie.

"What is this?"

"Put it in your laptop, and it'll pop up with all my information. It also has info about me running for junior class president. See you Monday."

I find Mom standing in the doorway of Mr. James's office, taking steps away, being drawn back, and finally breaking free with a look of relief on her face. "That was hard."

"What was?"

"Getting away from Mr. James."

We recite Mr. James quotes on the walk back to the car.

"You will just love this school," I say with enthusiasm.

"Our school has one of the highest academic ratings in not just the state of California but the nation as well."

"I think Mr. James is reliving his high school experience," Mom says in the voice she uses when she and Aunt Jenna do their people-watching/story-making game.

"Not reliving, recreating. I think he was a painfully awkward teenager."

We both laugh at that, and then Mom feels guilty for making fun of my school guidance counselor and says what a nice man Mr. James is and certainly an asset to the students who have him. "But you know," she says as we open the car doors, "Carson wouldn't have fit here at all."

That makes us silent. Neither of us speaks the entire drive home.

Once in my room, which is still a maze of boxes, I dial Carson's number. My friends are in school, but Carson gets out early for work experience. His voice mail comes on.

I leave a message: "I can't believe you deserted me! You need to call me soon."

I try my dad's house, then Carson's best friend, Marty's house, only to find out that Carson headed up to the mountains after school.

He's not ignoring me, I do know this. My brother is one of the least techie people to live in the twenty-first century. I created his MySpace for him. His friends often complain that they can't reach him, or he forgot to turn on his phone, or he let the battery go dead. If he'd been born several hundred years ago, Carson would be exploring the New World. That's my brother. And when life gets hard or stressed, he goes to the mountains.

So that's where he is now. Driving back roads, music on. Maybe he'll go for a long hike to one of his favorite lakes with a fishing pole in his backpack. I've gone with him a few times, and I follow the unspoken rules. We stop and get snacks; then he turns on some music, and we don't talk except on rare occasions. And there's something about driving those long mountain roads that gives a sense of freedom and escape and washes away the bad for a few hours.

Sometimes we talk on the drive home; other times we come back in continued silence as the reality of life returns. I rode with my brother after Dad told us he'd gotten married, and when Carson and his first girlfriend broke up, and again when Mom first told us about Aunt Betty giving us the house.

The boxes cluttering my room press in around me as I lie on my bed.

If Carson were here, I'd ask for a drive. I want my brother to be my brother still. With him there and me here, it's like suddenly we aren't siblings, or it's like he died but no one is really sad about it yet. Thinking of Carson dying reminds me of Little Tony.

My head feels foggy as I pull a blanket over me. Foggy and sad and thinking of Carson driving and driving on some mountain road and trying to remember exactly what Little Tony's face looked like—he had freckles, I remember, but what color were his eyes? What does it matter now that they will never look around the world again?

I wake to darkness with my cell phone vibrating next to my ear. It's Kate, which makes me realize that I never read her other texts.

KATE: So what did you think?
ME: I forgot to read it.
KATE: Hello?! Earth to Ruby.
ME: Was in a guidance counselor appt.
KATE: Yeah, yeah. K then, recap. Nick doesn't want to go
    with Nikki but feels bad telling her. He was caught
    off guard when she asked. It'd be so fun if you went

with him. We'll get a limo and go to dinner at Nello's
or . . .

ME: So you're going for sure?

KATE: Probably with Jeffers—as friends only.

ME: Hands Jeffers? I'll be your bodyguard.

KATE: Yes, though you might want to keep your attention
on your boyfriend.

ME: LOL, we're a bit presumptuous, aren't we?

KATE: Speak human please.

ME: Sorry. Hey, have you seen my brother?

KATE: Yeah. At school and at Marty's house when my
brother picked me up.

ME: What did he say?

KATE: I didn't really talk to him. But my brother said he'd
be crazy to move now with only one year left. He's
gone to school with everyone since kindergarten.

ME: Like me.

KATE: Like you.

ME: Tell him I keep trying to call him.

KATE: K. Sorry Rubes. But back to important—what do you
think about Nick?

chapter eight

I have this recurring daydream.

It's a secret to everyone except Kate.

The closest city to my hometown of Cottonwood is Redding. It's not a big city; it's just the only city within several hundred miles. According to my parents, who've lived there most of their lives, Redding has experienced a cultural awakening. They've renovated the downtown area and the old Cascade Theater and other stuff that adults get excited about. All I know is that Redding's mall is embarrassingly small.

But Redding has the coolest bridge I've ever seen. The Sundial Bridge.

From miles away, the massive white column of the bridge's dial is visible, rising from the trees like an airplane tail or a ship's sail frozen in motion. The walking bridge stretches over the wide Sacramento River, with the dial rising on the far side with thick cables in symmetric lines holding the dial to the bridge. If someone could see it from above, it really would look like one of those old Roman sundials. And it really works.

At the summer equinox on June 21, the shadow from the dial falls in perfect alignment with the time knobs on the ground. Mom took me one year to see it. The day was filled with local groups and musicians putting on sun-related festivities: sunspot viewing through giant telescopes, sun dances, and scientific games for kids. It was pretty fun.

But the bridge at night—that's when it's nearly magical in beauty.

If you cross the bridge and go down the trail that leads beneath the bridge, the huge cables that hold the dial look like a giant violin. But only at night and from this point of view. Also, the soft green glow that comes from the translucent glass reflects off the river below. In the summer, bands play at the little Turtle Bay Café, and there's a stillness to the diamond sky above us.

Not everyone loved the Sundial Bridge at first. Some people made fun of it—which, when I hear it, causes anger to rise in me and I want to call those people stupid or hicks or cultural losers. I'm not sure why I need to defend the bridge—it's a bridge! And so I remind myself that there were people against the construction of the Eiffel Tower in 1889. And what would Paris be without the Eiffel Tower? So Redding has its Sundial Bridge.

Anyway, back to my recurring daydream, or rather night dream or rainy night dream.

I'm at the Sundial Bridge at night when the stars are their brightest.

The soft green glow of light comes through the frosted glass walkway.

It's raining.

I'm there with *him*. The unknown *him* every girl imagines

and maybe someday finds, hopefully, though I don't see that many women with a husband who looks like *him*. (This worries me, I must admit.)

My *him* is there with me, though I can't see his face, but his presence is more familiar than anything that belongs to me. It's that familiarity I feel on rare moments among family—not those times when I'm sure I'm adopted or wonder why I can't be comfortable playing games, undistracted, and not like the black sheep of the family. Not those moments.

But the familiarity when I can wear anything, not even look in the mirror, and laugh as loud and long as I want. Something like that kind of comfortable knowing, but even more so. He, the mystery guy, is like a part of me, part of my future, but it feels like I've always known him too, and that we've always been a part of each other. Maybe that's where the idea of soul mates was born.

And so, okay, I'm reasonable enough to know this mystery guy may be all a dream and might always be. But I dream it anyway.

In the dream, we hold hands as our feet walk over the glow of soft green light going near the white railing above the rippling waters of the Sacramento River. The clouds hang low and offer the soft rain that dampens our hair and faces.

In some renditions, we sit beneath the covered area of the Turtle Bay Café and drink coffee or cocoa or hot tea, depending on what I'm in the mood for when I'm imagining. We lean close and talk about books, movies, and philosophy while warming our hands around our cups. Or we talk through our eyes, with silent mouths, as our fingers touch each other's.

Maybe we run across the bridge instead of strolling, and I

slip a little, a graceful slip, not my usual awkward stumble. He catches me and holds me close, breathing in the smell of my hair, and the smell of him fills my senses, and the scent that is him is also now me. For we're best friends times a thousand. Boyfriend/girlfriend times a million. Two lost halves, finally a whole.

Then, despite my variety of imaginings up to this moment, then we reach the moment. The final moment that is always the same.

One beautiful, perfect, solitary moment.

Here it is.

There in the soft light of the night, beneath cables like a giant's harp string, our faces and hair wet with the rain, he stops and folds me in close against his chest.

And we kiss.

We kiss one of those rarest of kisses. A *Princess Bride* kiss, a Klimt painting kiss, a *Notebook* kiss—yeah, that one even has rain like mine.

This kiss isn't like anything I've seen or experienced before or ever could with anyone else.

That is the bridge guy.

NICK: What have you been doing? You're gone a few days and then desert us? We need to talk, you and me.

ME: I suppose we do. I slept all Saturday, it's crazy how much I slept. Then I had to clean my room and my phone is being weird, and now I'm getting ready for

church. I just got online and everyone is suddenly
talking to me.
NICK: Excuses excuses.

A bunch of other messages are popping up as I type. This is
the first I've been on my laptop in my room since we arrived. My
e-mail and MySpace are filled with messages. I'm still loved,
which is nice to know when I wake in a strange room in a strange
town and it takes several minutes to even know where I am—
which happened twice last night.

"It's time for church!" Mom calls up the stairs.

I say good-bye to everyone with a promise to talk on the
phone with Nick later, then close my laptop and trudge downstairs.

Church? Moving, work, my counselor's appointment, sleeping all day yesterday, and this tiredness from moving and working
have kept me from responding to most everything my friends
have sent. I want to stay home in my pajamas, get a cup of coffee,
and catch up with everyone. But Mom is unrelenting.

Austin teases me about the frown on my face as we get in the
car, but I don't even care.

For the longest time, my feet were in Cottonwood but my
head was somewhere else. Now my feet are here in Marin—at the
moment they are resting on the floorboard of the car and are being
driven to church—but my head is very much in Cottonwood.

We're going to "try out" different churches. Mom and
Austin already went to one when they were down here a few
weeks ago. They said it was a "maybe," so we'll visit there soon.

We pull into a parking lot by a warehouse-looking place

with no landscaping outside, but lots of cars and people stream-ing in. It's the exact opposite of the church my parents attended when I was little and they were still married, with its hundred-year-old bell tower and white clapboard siding. Even the people walking in don't look like the usual churchgoers. No dresses and old ladies in nylons and pumps, not a suit jacket or tie in sight. These people look ready for a rock concert or an outdoor art fair.

"Leave your phone in the car," Mom says, and Austin gives me a smile.

"But—"

"For one hour every week, you can leave your phone."

"I have to leave my phone for more than one hour a week." I say this as I set my phone on the seat, where it looks sad and small next to the seat belt. "I don't have my phone while I work, when I sleep, or when I shower. And once in a while I go out without it."

"Wow," Mac says. "That's an accomplishment."

Mom and Austin laugh, which makes Mac smile like that kid from *Where the Wild Things Are*. I give him one of my looks.

This church is marketed toward the young, hip crowd. Mom and Austin keep glancing at each other, and I hear Mom whisper, "I think we're too old to be here."

It's pretty cool though. The worship music has a strong beat. There're guitarists, a keyboardist, and a drummer, and long lights dangle from the ceiling. The place sort of reminds me of a large, open Starbucks, and then I hear the hissing sound of milk steam-ing and spot the espresso section.

Mom closes her eyes during the worship songs. Mac sings

louder than I think he should, so finally I nudge him with my elbow, forgetting that it's in direct line with his head.

"Ouch!" he yells just as the melody pauses, bringing down raised arms and causing heads to turn our way like a wave of dominoes falling.

I want to sink and hide in the couch we're standing in front of. Mom doesn't notice, but Austin gives a little smile—my stepdad never gets annoyed at either of us, which is pretty nice considering stepdad stories—and the other faces quickly turn around and back toward the sky to the invisible God they all seek to worship.

Strangely, He—God, that is—feels very invisible to me. And I realize it's been a long time since I've thought of Him otherwise. Once He was as existent as the weather, a cool breeze on my face, or even as concrete in my life as . . . my cell phone. But of course more than that. He was God to me. Now it's like maybe I made all that up.

It sort of scares me to think this way. But I can't help but wonder as my heart rests still and empty within my chest if all these people are making God up for themselves as they raise their hands and weep and sing with such peace on their faces.

God, where did You go? Or are You even there?

The pastor speaks from a small platform in the center of the couches and chairs. He talks about "gratitude in the midst of . . ." He explains that "in the midst of" could be any circumstance, trial, temptation, or challenge.

He talks a lot about gratitude, and I draw little pictures on my program that make Mac smile, then we play tic-tac-toe and MASH.

When we get to the car, I find Kate has sent me a 911 text:

KATE: You MUST call me. ASAP!
ME: Why?
KATE: Nick news.
ME: I'll call when I get home.

But strangely, I don't really care to call or know the big secret. A week ago I would've been dying to find out, but now the anxiety and excitement are gone. I can guess what it'll be about—Nick wishes he could take me to prom, Nikki found out and now she doesn't want to go with him, Kate and my friends will want me to go with Nick, Nikki will be mad at me, my friends mad at her . . . the usual drama.

As we eat tacos at a little restaurant that is my new favorite Mexican restaurant of all time—this decided as soon as I taste the best salsa ever and view an interior so authentic that I expect to walk outside and find ourselves in MAYheeco—Austin asks, "So what did you think of the church?"

"It was cool, I guess." Something about being at church, even with my scary questions about God, gave me a surprising peace that I've brought along to the Mexican restaurant.

"I'm not sure if *cool* is good or bad," Austin says with a laugh.

Austin isn't as outgoing as my dad, who could make friends with a lamppost. But he's genuine, trustworthy, and . . . steady. That's something I didn't realize was important until our fractured family didn't have it. Mom can be cluttered with too many thoughts, too many things to do, and too many worries. She cooks, cleans, and organizes when she's worried about us—which has been all the time lately. When she's relaxed, Mom is a fun mom who also offers great advice. Austin says he was pretty boring without Mom, so I guess they even each other out.

We're still a pretty fractured family, I realize, thinking of Carson, who still hasn't even called me. But at least we don't have to worry about Mom the way we did for a while. Carson would come in my room at night, upset that she wouldn't get out of bed or eat much, that she looked dazed and confused and was missing her article deadlines and not paying the bills.

"I guess there's a lot to be grateful for," I say, but I keep thinking how Carson isn't with us—and he'd so love the super burrito they have here—and how Dad is far away and living his life, and how I don't have any friends and am starting at a school like Little Orphan Annie going to a New York prep academy. But I make Mom and Austin smile by saying, "I'm grateful for this taco, even in the midst of . . ."

I should have cared about what Kate wanted to tell me.

Sometimes I don't believe her 911 texts.

But the Nick news was more urgent than I expected.

When I called her hours later, she said, "You are too late again! Answer your phone and get with it, sister!"

So Nikki found out that Nick planned to take me to the prom. Nikki is mad at me, my friends are mad at her, but she will not let Nick out of his promise to go with her. Nick asked Kate to ask me if I for sure would go to the prom with him if he dumped Nikki. He tried calling me several times—suddenly he's bold enough not only to admit to liking me, but to expect me to attend the prom with him before he's even asked me directly. I usually find self-confidence attractive, but this weight of something, like a giant backpack strapped to my back, steals away any excitement or attraction.

My social life is being tugged to and fro by the forces of people hundreds of miles away.

I'm tired. As in, so tired.

And so Nikki called Nick, and without a direct answer from me, he had to reconfirm that he would indeed attend the prom with her. I'm out again, though I didn't really know I was in.

I care about this—I really do like Nick a lot—but it's all somewhere deep down inside of me, so deep that my head keeps reminding my heart that it cares, it really cares. And tomorrow is my first day at the new school.

chapter nine

"Hey, New Girl," someone calls behind me.

I've been at Marin High half a day, and I know without a doubt that I hate it here.

It's a huge school. I needed the map they gave me in my student packet, especially since Lucinda didn't meet me outside the campus office like she said. I definitely won't be voting for her for anything, ever.

This guy started following me soon after lunch. Lunch, which was a disaster consisting of me wandering around and hoping no one noticed the lost new girl—and then, of course, this guy did.

"Hey, slow down," he says, coming up beside me. He's a jock. Football jersey, buzzed haircut, baseball cap, cool jock shoes. He's like a thousand times jock; it oozes from his pores.

"What makes you think I'm new?" There are hundreds of students, so I can't understand how I'm so easy to identify.

"You're carrying a map and actually looking at it." He smiles a jock half smile. I really like it when Nick smiles that way, but not this cocky guy.

"Oh." I keep walking.

"Come on, wait a minute, New Girl."

Without turning or pausing, I duck into the girls' bathroom. The clean walls inside the stall offer nothing to read, which at this moment is a little disappointing. Guess I'll be bored the rest of the day, since I'm not leaving this stall. Ever.

Something's wrong with my cell phone. The battery was dead by second period. This phone is ancient—I've had it for over a year.

Leaning against the door, I look at my schoolbooks. In less than five minutes, I'm bored. I'm really going to need a new phone. I stare at its sad dead screen, willing it to come to life. Then I formulate reasons to miss school the rest of the week. Or year.

Mom, I feel sick.

The kids are mean to me.

I think I have cancer.

Or the one that would work without fail, but I'd feel too guilty to use it: "I keep thinking about the divorce and how our life was before . . ." Nix that one.

I have cramps, really bad ones.

I'm having anxieties.

Someone told me there's going to be a school shooting.

The last one is the best, but then I imagine Mom freaking out, calling the police, the school going into lockdown, me interviewed in a cold interrogation room for ten hours without food or water until I finally confess that I just didn't want to go to school. I wonder if you can get prison time for that.

I could be homeschooled. There're only four months left of this year anyway.

Or I could go back to Cottonwood . . .

The bell rings and I leave the bathroom stall, glancing both ways outside the door for Super Jock, then onward to fifth-period English. I'm late even with my trusty and humiliating map.

I sit down, and someone behind me says, "Isn't that the girl from the Underground?"

It's better than New Girl.

I turn in my seat and meet Frankie's wide smile, a smile that makes me smile too. And I ask myself the perennial question—why are the cutest guys gay?

"Ruby, right?" he says.

"Yes. Frankie, right?"

The teacher tells the class to turn to a section of *Julius Caesar* and asks me to come forward to get a book and study guide.

After class, Frankie sets his gray bag on my desk. "So how's assimilation?"

"Huh?"

"Adjusting to Marin High?"

"Uh, well, about as good as adjusting to Marin in general."

"It can be a rough crowd."

I nod slowly. "Yes, but not rough as in if I moved to Chino." I say Chino because it's the only ganglike town I've heard of . . . from watching *The OC*.

"Oh, it's just as rough. Surviving the Paris and Nicole types can be as treacherous as surviving an African war zone. There are rich kids who will never need to work a day in their lives, and also brilliant people already working toward their Nobel Prizes.

But a normal girl like you, you stick out like . . . like something that really sticks out."

"Normal, huh? I've become normal." In Cottonwood I was artistic, intelligent, unique—someone who didn't fit with the athletes or ranchers. I've descended into normality.

"Bad choice of words. I reserve the right to withdraw. What I meant is that you're the all-American girl. No airs of pretension. You're like a brunette Reese Witherspoon. A girl bands write songs about. Not hip-hop, R&B, metal, or rap songs, mind you. But something Bryan Adams, Springsteen, Tom Petty—"

"I'm the type of girl that old, outdated guys would sing about?"

This guy is digging a hole.

"No, no. And even if they're older, they aren't outdated— never say that. The young ones sing about girls like you. Justin Timberlake, and I'm sure a lot of others. I tend to like older music. You work at a coffeehouse, with that wide smile on your face, happy as can be. You probably go to church—a Christian church—and I bet your parents aren't even divorced."

"Got the divorce part wrong. And I'm not always happy."

"Well, don't let this crazy smattering of people get you down, American girl. You're what men go off to war over, what makes this country great, what people cheer for at the Olympics."

"Oh my word!"

"Exactly. Who says, 'Oh my word!'"

I laugh at that.

"We should go for coffee. I'll buy. And maybe I should make it too." He makes a face.

"I've greatly improved my espresso-making skills."

His exaggerated expression of disbelief makes me laugh again.
"It was that bad, huh?" I ask.
"Girlfriend, that was the worst coffee I've ever tasted."
And just like that, I have a friend.

Mom picks me up after school—we're unsure how I'll get home now that Carson isn't coming, and I'm praying I won't have to ride the bus. And then, gift of all gifts, Mom drives me to the phone store. Instead of a new battery, she uses her free upgrade to get me a new phone, and I'm so happy that I tell Mom I love her and kiss her cheek.

I don't tell her any of my excuses or how miserable I was at school. Frankie did improve the day, but I still don't want to return.

My phone is lime green—it would match that dress—with all the features.

A text comes in. The first on my cute new phone.

KATE: What was it like?
ME: The school is amazing. They have an espresso bar.
    They have nearly every art class you can think of.
KATE: Pottery?
ME: Funny.

Kate never lets me forget my many art forays and foibles. She particularly loves to remind me that I was nearly kicked out of pottery class. Let's just say that wheel can be very dangerous.

KATE: Serious. It takes real skill to launch a clay cannonball through a window and just miss the principal.

ME: Enough already.

KATE: I forgot to tell you! This was in one of my super important texts you missed.

ME: Nick news again?

KATE: No, Kate news.

ME: Tell me!

KATE: I'm coming down in two weeks.

ME: Two weeks? REALLY!!!!

KATE: Yeah, cool huh? My mom is visiting my aunt in Santa Rosa for the weekend. She already talked to your mom about it.

ME: I'm so happy. We'll have so much fun.

KATE: Are there tons of cute guys?

Me: Yeah, I have seen a lot. And I made a friend.

KATE: Girl or guy?

ME: Guy.

KATE: Reeeealllly?

ME: Yeah, but it's not like that.

KATE: Reeeeealllly, so what's it like then?

ME: He's gay.

KATE: Oh. Bummer. I suppose he's totally hot too.

ME: Of course.

KATE: Well, you'll have someone to go shopping with. That is, till I get there.

ME: He'll be my substitute Kate.

KATE: Don't make me jealous now. Hey I saw your brother today.

ME: Did you tell him I'm mad at him?

KATE: Yes. He said Oh.

ME: Sounds like Carson.

A different beep sounds from the one that identifies Kate's texts. I open, and it's Frankie.

FRANKIE: Are you working tonight, little working girl?

RUBY TO KATE: Hang on sec Kate, it's Frankie.

KATE: It's happening already.

ME TO FRANKIE: Normal Girl has today off, not working till Thurs.

FRANKIE: Ouch, normal girl eh? I didn't mean it like that.

ME: Uh-huh.

FRANKIE: Subject change. Tell me impressions of Marin.

ME: I thought I did.

FRANKIE: No, no, no, girl. Impressions. What does it give off to you. It's the artEEst in me to know these things. Give it a title?

ME: Explain title.

FRANKIE: Every place, every person has a title. What's Marin's title. Wealth and Culture by the Sea?

ME: That's good. Or maybe . . . Liberal Politics and Green by the Bay?

FRANKIE: There you go.

These are not words I would have used last week in Cottonwood. Liberal politics meant nothing to me. Politics in general was of little interest to me. My entire family and most of the people I know are conservative Republicans or conservative Democrats or nonpolitical. Here the political climate is alive and discussed around steaming cups of chai and organic hot chocolate.

> ME: A customer asked what I thought of some issue. I said I'm not political and he said I shouldn't have the freedom to live here. That I'm irresponsible.
> FRANKIE: Ouch.
> ME: His wife reminded him I'm a teenager. He said that's the best time to become informed.
> FRANKIE: I'm about as political as Hannah Montana.
> ME: Hannah Montana?
> FRANKIE: Yeah, I love that show! That girl's got it going on. So what is your title?
> ME: Mine?
> FRANKIE: Yep.
> ME: Uh . . .

Kate pops in here, and I think I should get online and make this all easier on myself, though I'm quickly getting adjusted to the keypad on my new phone.

> KATE: HELLO????
> ME TO FRANKIE: Guess I'd have to think on it.
> ME TO KATE: Sorry. What were we talking about?
> KATE: Uh-huh.
> FRANKIE: Go with the first thing that comes to your head. Some things you are or feel. Go.

For a moment, I think to tease him again about calling me Normal Girl, or I could bring up New Girl or the many nicknames my family and friends have created. But then I just try this little self-exploration.

> ME: Wanderer, seeker, lover of art, new arrival—yeah, that was dumb.
> FRANKIE: What else? Whatever comes to mind, nothing is dumb.
> ME: Um, bridges, joyful, lonely, lost, missing my brother and dad, confused, sadness, truth, God, real, missing something, wanting home and wanting adventure, or greatness, not greatness, but something like that.
> FRANKIE: Girl, if I were straight, I'd date you.
> ME: O-kay.
> FRANKIE: Hey now, that's a compliment.
> ME: Yeah, but it's like my mom saying I'm the prettiest girl in the world.
> FRANKIE: LOL. Wide-Eyed Innocence Steps Out into the Great Big World.
> ME: Hmm, I can live with that. What's your title?
> FRANKIE: Sexiest Man Alive.
> ME: Perfect.
> FRANKIE: Don't I know that. If only the world did.

Frankie has to go at the same time I'm called down to dinner.

I walk down the stairs to the sound of classical music and the scent of garlic and pasta sauce with a hint of fresh paint in the background.

Mac calls through the archway that leads to the dining room, "Austin cooked pasta and a bunch of stuff. We're having dinner at the table tonight."

"I have tons of homework."

Dinner at the table together is sometimes annoying, even though I understand why everyone else enjoys it. I like eating in my room or standing up in the kitchen or sitting behind the coffee table watching TV.

Austin usually goes all out when it's his turn to cook. With Mom it might be pizza, or bacon and eggs, or some gourmet experiment—that sometimes goes wrong. But Austin's meals are right-on dependable and delicious. We'd be fat and poor if he cooked regularly.

Mac's wearing the "man apron," as he calls it, and setting linen napkins around the set table. Boxes line the walls of the dining room, but the table looks like we're having a holiday with candles lit and garden flowers laid along the center.

"Austin said it didn't matter what everyone was doing, that we could all take a half hour to be together. We all get to tell two things about our day."

"Gee, great."

He says with the seriousness of a ten-year-old, "So go wash up; it's almost ready."

"Don't tell me what to do." But I head up the stairs toward the upstairs bathroom after seeing the downstairs one barricaded with house stuff.

"Be careful using the bathroom," Mom says from her room. "The walls are still wet. And I want to work on decorating your room this weekend and getting your bathroom fixed up. So don't make too many plans."

"Oh, you don't need to worry about that," I say under my breath. My bathroom is a box-encased maze, so I wash my hands in the hall bathroom.

"We should do a theme in your room," Mom calls. "Maybe black and white, with a Paris theme."

"How about Croatian?" I say, thinking of Natasha.

Mom peers out her bedroom door, and I see that she's changed her clothes, put on makeup, and added some curl to her shoulder-length brown hair for this, our special dinner event. Honestly, I just want to get online and talk to my friends, or ignore them and talk to Frankie all night. No one else makes me think of such odd but interesting things.

Mom gives me a strange expression. "You want your room Croatian? Like Croatia, the country that was part of former Yugoslavia?"

"Yeah, or someplace exotic like that."

"Uh, okay. Sure, we'll go for exotic. We're going to paint Carson's room too."

"I want Carson's room!"

"You can have his room when you go to college. It's not a good idea for you to be outside like that."

"It's a good idea to me."

"Yes, I know."

"So why are you working on Carson's room?"

"He might change his mind someday, and I want him to feel comfortable when he comes down. He could bring friends."

I nod but feel sad for Mom suddenly. I decide to be more engaged in our "family night." I even leave my phone upstairs.

Over plates of pasta, salad, and the best sourdough bread I think I've ever had, we go around and say two things about our day. I want to roll my eyes at how excited Mac is about this. If Carson were here, he'd probably have that look on his face that says, *You've got to be kidding—you are* not *making me do this.* But then Mom would get him to say something, even if it's a sarcastic "The best part of my day is being here with all of you, my loving family." Which would make us all laugh.

The empty chair beside me makes me miss him all the more.

Mac says, "Well, I like my school. I made a bunch of new friends. They placed me in a math class with all sixth graders, and I played soccer at recess and almost made a goal."

I've been so wrapped up in my own world, I'd forgotten that the little guy was facing the same thing I faced today.

Mom and Austin say things about work, their new home, being together . . . the usual parental offerings. Then it's my turn.

"I got a new cell phone today, thank you very much, Mom. And I made one new friend," I say with enunciations like a little girl. "His name is Frankie, and he's very nice."

"That's great, honey."

And then I blurt, "And he's gay."

"Ew, gross," Mac says.

Mom and Austin look at each other. Then Mom says, "Okay. But was that necessary to include?"

"Guess not." I laugh nervously. "Just thought I'd get that out of the way before you meet him and are surprised, or before you worry that I'll like him. Aunt Jenna knows him and likes him."

"O-kay," Mom says, and I know her mind is trying to settle on what she thinks of all this.

"Ew, that's so gross. He kisses boys!"

Mac starts making gagging noises, and I mouth "Sorry" to Mom for disrupting the otherwise family-perfect dinner.

Dinner doesn't last much longer than that, though Mom and Austin remain at the table as I hurry upstairs and back to my social life. As I turn on my computer, I suddenly remember Kate. I left her hanging hours ago, when I was talking to Frankie. I totally forgot about her.

Oh, she's going to be mad.

chapter ten

FRANKIE: What color are you?

ME: Huh?

FRANKIE: Do you know how often you say that?

ME: Say what?

FRANKIE: HUH?

ME: You ask me the strangest questions.

FRANKIE: And you love them so much. You think about them later in the day while you're serving coffee and pumpkin bread. Admit it.

ME: I do. Aquamarine.

FRANKIE: Aquamarine? That's not a color.

ME: Yes it is. If it's in a Crayola box, it's a color. What's yours?

FRANKIE: Red, of course. Flamboyant Red though I don't think Crayola has that. Why, ick, aquamarine?

ME: I don't know. For once I'm giving an answer off the top of my head instead of thinking it over all day,

while I'm serving coffee and pumpkin bread. Maybe
it's orange. Autumn is my favorite time of year, and I
was thinking of painting one of my bedroom walls
orange.

I look at the wall behind my bed and try imagining it a dark
orange color. It's late evening, and I'm still wearing my Underground
polo shirt, and my homework books from Day 2 at Marin High
surround me. Sepia-colored prints of places around the world
would go well on a dark orange wall.

My laptop chimes as friends keep talking to me online. I
comment back here and there, but Frankie is definitely the most
interesting of the bunch. Kate's at the movies with some people
I don't know very well, and though she says she forgives me for
forgetting her yesterday, it obviously hurt her feelings. And who
can blame her? I can tell it'll take her awhile to get over it.

My phone vibrates on the desk beside me—Frankie again.

FRANKIE: So you need to think about your color.
    Aquamarine is not it.
ME: I'll give you an answer by tomorrow.
FRANKIE: What were you before?
ME: Huh?
FRANKIE: See, huh again!
ME: LOL
FRANKIE: It changes you know. Life turns us different colors
    for different times in our lives. There was a time I was
    gray, a dark charcoal gray for a very long time.
ME: Ah, yes, I think I've seen myself as gray.

FRANKIE: So ready to see the town?

ME: Huh? Okay, I'll stop saying that.

FRANKIE: Tell me where you're at, and I'll take you round.

ME: Not sure I can. I have homework. Julius Caesar and
     logarithms.

FRANKIE: I won't have you out long.

ME: Hang on.

FRANKIE: Oh right, American Girl must ask permission
     from Mommy.

I race down the stairs with my phone in hand to find Mom, and I wonder what I believe about homosexuality. And then I wonder why I'm wondering about this right now. But still, I know what most Christians think, what my dad and my grandmother would say. Grandma Hazel will start sending me Bible tracts if she hears I have a gay friend. And I know what the extreme conservative Christians have projected on gay people—that they should be hated, that they are evil. Mom gets really upset about people like that and sometimes goes on a rampage, saying she's going to write all these articles or a book about it. Our pastor in Cottonwood preached a sermon about it; he says love them, don't condemn or judge them as we shouldn't condemn or judge anyone, treat them as Jesus would treat anyone, look at the sin in our own lives, etc.

Between my room and the living room, I decide that I don't really care to figure it all out right now.

Mom is working on her laptop at the coffee table, with Mac doing his homework beside her.

"We're working here. Don't interrupt, please," Mac says and then smiles at me.

"My new friend wants to pick me up."

Mom gets that look—eyebrows pinched together and a slight frown. "Why don't you guys just hang out here?" She glances at Austin, who's in a chair reading the paper.

"He wants to give me a driving tour of the area."

Mom shakes her head. "No. We have to meet him first."

ME: They said no.
Frankie: I'll talk to them.
ME: You don't know my mom.
FRANKIE: She's a tyrant?
ME: No. But she can be strict.
FRANKIE: Parents love me. Or let me rephrase. Moms love
    me. Dads and brothers, not so much.
ME: I wonder why.
FRANKIE: I can't figure it out.

Then Austin says, "You should let her go. After we meet him."

Mom looks at Austin. "What? Why?"

"She needs some friends," he says.

Mom is quiet a moment, then says, "Okay, but after we meet him."

Stepdad saves the night.

Mac peeks at Frankie from the top of the stairs, and I give him an angry wave to go away. I hear his laugh as he hurries off to his room, probably both disgusted and fascinated at my "boy-kissing" friend. I'm just glad Carson isn't here right now.

"Hello, Frankie," Mom says, coming out of the kitchen. "Did you have dinner?"

"Yeah, I've already eaten. Penne pasta and white wine mushroom sauce."

"Yum," Austin says, coming in behind Mom. He shakes Frankie's hand, and I make the introductions.

"Well, it's Lean Cuisine. I'm a frozen dinner connoisseur. Gotta keep the figure lean and mean."

Before they can respond, Frankie starts asking question after question about the house. "It's one of the coolest houses I think I've ever seen," he says after getting the history and gazing around.

Austin even shows him the garage with the arched door and access to the backyard where the fruit trees are blooming. They like Frankie, just as he predicted.

"So you're going to show Ruby around?"

"Yep, it sounded like she needs to get out. And I promise to drive your daughter carefully, and I promise, really promise, that I won't kiss her."

That shocks me, but Mom chuckles. "It's nice to know she's safe then." She keeps laughing quietly as she follows us toward the door.

"Ew, kissing, gross!" I hear from Mac upstairs, and I want to slink away to my room.

But nothing fazes Frankie.

"Sorry about my brother," I say after the friendly good-byes and Mom's invitation for Frankie to come to dinner sometime—when Austin is cooking, she says with a laugh.

"Cute kid. Now ready to see some of Marin?"

We drive the hilly streets up one side of the mountain to the other where the rough Pacific waters beat against the cliffs.

Frankie chain-smokes but doesn't offer me one. He drives with the window cracked and holds a cigarette like someone from a movie, cool and casual-like. It almost makes me want to start smoking. He finally parks at a place that overlooks the water, with the sunset faded into the water and nearly turned to darkness. And for some reason, I tell him about little Tony Arnold in the Christmas program with me and now dead from a drug overdose.

We get out and walk barefoot on the beach, and Frankie strips down to his boxers and goes running to the water. I laugh as he jumps the waves and finally goes diving in. That water is freezing! But as I watch Frankie swim alone in the ocean, a sense of contented solitude surrounds me. A sense of knowing that this is the time and place for me.

It's not Frankie in particular or the rhythm of waves or the bright moon coming up behind us as the last light disappears out across the ocean. There are plenty of troubles in this new life. But a gentle strength reminds me that I'm going forward in life's pathway, and nothing in the world needs to stop me now.

chapter eleven

I don't have to wander the lunch periods alone anymore, like the first day when I bought a sandwich and then moved from place to place as if I had somewhere to go. If anyone had actually been watching me, I'd have appeared pretty ridiculous.

Today is the second day Frankie has lunch with me, but this time he brings me to his table of friends. Before moving to Marin, people like Bart, Axner, and Janice might have freaked me out a little with their tattoos and piercings. Bart is the size of a small giant and wears all black and black eyeliner. Axner is short and stares at me intensely, then smiles widely and shakes my hand. Janice gives me a cool nod of welcome, then rests her head back on Bart's shoulder. Another guy and girl arrive at the table.

"This is Redden. My gay brother, but not my gay lover," Frankie says in a singsong voice, and they high-five.

"Nice to meet you," I say awkwardly, not sure how to respond to Frankie's flamboyance sometimes. Is the guy really his brother, or just called that 'cause he's gay too?

"So, Frankie, this is your experiment into conservative

Americana," says a girl who just arrived. She's a hard and cold mix of beautiful.

"This is Blair. Blair, be nice to my Ruby."

"It won't be easy," Blair says and gives me a long condescending look that moves up and down my body.

Blair continues to make rude comments and references to me throughout lunch. I wonder what she has against me, and decide to ask Frankie later. And just as I now have one friend, I get the idea that I now have an enemy too.

Aunt Jenna picks me up from school, and we go straight to the Underground. I write Kate on my way to the coffeehouse, but she doesn't answer.

My twelve-hour day last week (was it only last week?) and working yesterday provide a comfortable familiarity. I've learned the espresso recipes and even get a few compliments. Some of the regulars know my name, which makes me try harder to remember theirs. I look for Natasha, but she doesn't come in today. When someone orders the pumpkin bread, I think of Frankie. *What color am I?* Who asks questions like that? He's one of the most unusual people I've ever met—and I love him for that.

ME: I think I'm purple.

I write to Frankie when I get home, once again so tired that it's hard to walk up the stairs to my room. I have homework and I'm hungry, but I know I need to talk to Kate before I sleep.

ME TO KATE: Can you talk?

KATE: So you don't like Nick now?

ME: Yeah, I do.

Something's up with Kate, though her words make me realize that I haven't so much as asked about Nick in two days. And I never called him like I said I would. There was something Kate was going to tell me about him, and I never even asked.

ME TO KATE: It's not easy fitting in here and keeping up
        with the old.

FRANKIE: Purple huh? Like Prince or Barney the dinosaur.

ME TO FRANKIE: Purple like me.

FRANKIE: Hmmm. You know purple is sometimes
        considered the gay color.

ME: Well, not that purple either.

FRANKIE: Is there something wrong with gay purple?

ME: Uh, I didn't mean anything by that.

FRANKIE: LOL. Kidding. So what are you up to, Purple?
        You're going to have to explain that by the way.

ME: Unpacking my room, starting homework, and talking
        to friends online.

FRANKIE: Busy busy.

I take a drink of Diet Pepsi and accidentally push a book and school papers that fall behind the desk. It takes wedging my feet against the wall and pulling to budge the heavy desk from the wall. As I pick up the papers, I notice that a board on the back of the desk is loose, with an edge of something sticking out of the bottom of the board. I carefully pull out an old photograph. It shows a woman sitting on a stone fence with the sea in the background.

I write to Frankie and forward to Kate:

ME: I just found a really old photograph behind my
    aunt's desk.
KATE: Cool. So you aren't going to say anything about
    what I said?
ME: What did you say?
RE-SENT FROM KATE: So we're the old? All of us in
    Cottonwood are the old and it's too hard keeping up
    with us?
ME: Oh! I didn't mean that. Knock it off. You know I
    didn't mean it that way.
FRANKIE: An old photograph in your aunt's desk? Maybe
    auntie has a dirty little secret.
ME TO FRANKIE: It's an old photograph, like at least fifty
    years. And don't talk about my aunt that way.
FRANKIE: Oh, a mystery for Nancy Drew. Hey, you could
    be Nancy Drew, that's a good title for you.
ME TO KATE & FRANKIE: On the back it says To my
    beloved Beatrice. This one photograph I release from
    my collection to you. Thank you for coming to the
    shoot that day by the sea. May the future hold such
    wonder as our days in France. Yours always, E
KATE: Cool.

That's about all the interest those two have in the photograph.

As if they are the same person. I smile to myself as I consider that.

Kate and Frankie have to go at the same time. I'm distracted over the picture, staring at the woman's face—she's quite beautiful in that old-fashioned way—and wondering who she is.

I realize after she says good-bye just how strange Kate has been acting during our conversations. She must be mad at me, and I'll need to address that soon. Though usually she'll outright tell me she's angry. Quick and unexplained good-byes aren't like her.

I try to focus on my WWI workbook questions while only occasionally talking to one friend or another. Mostly it's the same catching up on the same details of Cottonwood: someone was in a fight and it's the big scandal, Randy is going to enter a snowboarding competition, Alisha's boyfriend is cheating on her but she doesn't believe it, Nikki picked out a yellow dress and Nick refuses to get a yellow tie for prom (and he still wants to talk to me, but I've been avoiding that conversation), Felicity agreed to go to the prom with Josh though she really wants to go with Harlen . . . stuff like that.

I keep looking at the photograph. It's distracting me from the 1918 assassination of Austrian Archduke Franz Ferdinand by a Bosnian Serb student in Yugoslavia. Finally I run downstairs with the picture in my hand.

"Mom, do you know a Beatrice or someone with the initial *E*?"

She's working on her laptop, sitting on the couch with papers spread all around her. The fire crackles, and part of me thinks to come downstairs and do my homework at the coffee table near her.

"Uh, *E*? There's Ernest Hemingway," she says, her eyes not moving from the screen. Her reading glasses are inching down her nose.

"I mean in our family. Or someone Aunt Betty would know."

"Hmm. Aunt Betty's name is actually Beatrice. Why?"

"Mom, Mom!" Mac comes running from outside. "Ruby, Ruby!"

"What, what!" I say.

"Come out here quick. You need to see this guy."

Mom and I give each other a knowing look and sigh, then get up and hurry to the front door. Just then a guy makes a circle and waves, riding a sort of motorized unicycle with a headlight and what appears to be a solar panel rising above him on a metal bar. He tips his hat at my stare and is gone before I can wave back or smile or respond at all.

"Only in Marin," Mom says.

Back inside, I show Mom the picture. She studies it and reads the back. "This is interesting."

"Do you think this is Aunt Betty?" It's strange to imagine my quirky old aunt as this young, thoughtful woman.

"The photograph looks like it's from around the fifties or maybe older. So it could be her."

"Did she go to France when she was young?"

Mom sits back on the couch and picks up her laptop, then pauses. "You know, I think there was some scandal with Aunt Betty when she was in her early twenties. She ran off to Europe or something. We'll have to ask her when she returns. If she'll tell us."

I survive Day 4 of Marin High.

Lunch with Frankie and his friends helps a lot, except for Blair.

"So you're a Christian?" she asks with a short laugh.

For a second, I hesitate. Usually I might be embarrassed or intimidated by such a question, but she makes me want to fight back. "Yeah."

"And why would that be? Why are you a Christian?"

Frankie comes to my rescue. "What are you, Blair, darling?"

"I'm Blair. I believe in me," she says with confidence, and the conversation thankfully goes another direction.

Then I see Super Jock across the quad. He followed me around earlier, again calling, "Hey, New Girl." When he sees me sitting with Frankie and friends, a surprised expression comes over his face. I think he'll leave me alone now.

A strange pride surrounds me as I sit with Frankie and friends at lunch. Maybe it's that I'm hanging out with the kind of people I'd be terrified to sit with before. Maybe it's just that I'm no longer sitting alone.

Hours later, when I arrive at work, I see a check with my name on it. My first job, my first check. It's for $87.50 after taxes. I want to kiss it and jump up and down. Instead I slide it into my purse and get my apron, already picking out things to spend it on.

Ruby Unscripted

The first three hours of work slide by. My favorite trio of old men is there, as usual. They sit around talking about their most recent marathons or news and politics or their aches and pains. And they love flirting with me, which is quite humorous since they're certainly all over seventy.

I'm cleaning beneath a small table where a cute little kid made a very uncute mess when I hear some girls talking at a table nearby.

"I've seen her before," I hear someone say.

Wet globs of cracker are stuck to the table legs. The girls are looking at me. Do they really think I can't hear them from only three tables away?

"She just moved here from some hick town."

"How do you know?"

"My mom knows her aunt. She wanted me to be friends with her or something."

I hit my head on the table but keep cleaning.

"Her name is Amethyst or Emerald or something like that."

"It's Ruby," I say, finally standing. "Can I take any of those plates for you?"

"Ruby—that's like an old, old, old-fashioned name," one girl says. She's blonde, beautiful—the stereotype for all those mean girls in every teen movie known to mankind.

I say, with the nicest of smiles, "Yes. Or Ruby for the slippers that Dorothy wore."

She laughs with a mocking tone. "There's no place like home, there's no place like home. So, Dorothy, isn't it true that the customer is always right?" She glances at her friends with a superior air.

"I'm sure that depends on the business."

"So does your boss tell you that the customer is always right?"

"Is there a problem?" I'm trying to take the lead from Aunt Jenna and only show cheeriness, and boy, it's harder than it looks.

One of her friends is hiding her laughter behind her hand.

Another girl nudges her and says, "Leave her alone. Come on, guys, let's go."

"I have a complaint. My mocha is cold."

It really is like one of those teen movies where the beautiful rich girls are picking on the normal girl who will someday rise above them all, get the cutest guy in the school, be voted homecoming queen . . . It's exactly like one of those—I hope. And somehow because it is so unreal, movielike, I find it completely comical, really, so wildly humorous and stereotypical . . .

And so I laugh.

It's not just a chuckle, not even from the start.

It's a true-blue guffaw.

The girl's mouth drops. Actually, all of them at the table look at me with expressions of shock, which makes me laugh all the more.

The girl stands so fast her chair falls over, which increases my laughter. She scoops up her Gucci purse and glares at me.

I sputter between my tears, "I'm sorry. It's not about you, really. It's just—"

"Let's get out of here. You're a freak," she spits.

Two girls stand, but the others remain.

"Are you guys coming? London?"

"No, I'm gonna hang here awhile longer. I'll catch up with you later."

The girl London was the one who told the mean girl to leave me alone.

I try going back to cleaning up tables, but I can't stop laughing. I turn away from the group, doing that silent laugh thing where your body shakes and any second you'll burst out and cause unknown havoc.

"Your employee is bad for business," the girl calls out to my aunt.

I realize Aunt Jenna has witnessed the whole scene.

"I know," she says with a wink at me.

The hours pass quickly after that. Near closing, I go downstairs in search of plates or cups left behind. In the main theater, I look up at the screen for a moment and breathe in the faint scent of popcorn. I have always loved the movies. This might be the first time I've been in a theater alone though. I sit down and lean back in the chair.

"Hey, could you get the lights?" someone calls behind me, and I jump to my feet.

"I thought everyone was gone." I can't see the guy in the projection area.

"Not yet. Your aunt said I could work on this till you close up."

"How do you know she's my aunt?"

"Do you mind? The lights?"

"Oh, okay." I find the switch by the door.

"Thanks," he says.

The screen shows a still and silent forest, then explodes soundlessly to the red fabric of a woman's dress. The title *Souvenirs* flashes like a neon sign coming on as the woman runs silently through the forest, and then the image freezes on the wall-sized screen.

"What does that look like in the left-hand corner?"

At first I don't see anything. Then I notice what appears to be a boy's face from behind one of the trees. When I say so, I hear a long, exasperated sigh.

"Guess I'll have to reshoot or cut him out."

"Why?"

"A film with a Peeping Tom in the woods wasn't what I was going for. And I thought I was done with this." He makes a frustrated sound.

"Only someone really looking will see it. And maybe it foreshadows something else in the story. Or it's like the boy is a ghost or, I don't know, something . . ."

Silence.

"Or you can reshoot or cut it," I say quickly.

And then he walks up beside me, looking at the face in the trees with interest, and I'm stunned to realize it's that guy. The cute one I saw coming from the kitchen on Premiere Night. The yard and moving guy. Kaden something.

"Might just work," he says, still staring. He stands there for several minutes as if he's forgotten I'm even there. Then he goes to the lights and flips them back on. "Your aunt and uncle talk a lot about you. As do your mom and stepdad."

"And what do they say about me?" I smile as I say this.

"A lot. They're great people though. You're lucky to have a family like that."

What do I say to that? "Yeah, I guess."

"So what's your experience?"

"Experience?"

"Film?" he says as if I should know what he meant.

"Uh, not much. I took a screenwriting workshop once." I'm actually sputtering as I talk. *Get it together, Ruby.*

"And what have you done with it?"

"I worked on a few screenplays, then I got distracted when some friends wanted to start a band."

"How'd that work out?"

I laugh, but he still waits for an answer with all seriousness.

"Since none of us was very advanced on any instrument, and we weren't very musical . . . let's just say I moved on to pottery after that."

"You're not very consistent, are you?"

I stand up, and the theater seat folds back loudly. "I just haven't found my niche yet."

"Sometimes you have to work hard and have it find you." He doesn't say this in a very kind or understanding way. I don't know that I like this guy.

"Yeah, maybe."

"Try sticking with one thing. I bet you've bounced around in sports and arts for years—maybe you're even adequate in a lot of things, but I bet you haven't truly applied yourself to be excellent at anything." He moves back toward the projection area and carries out a large case.

Crossing my arms at my chest, I clear my throat. After the mean girl incident today, I'm not going to cower to this guy. "I bet you heard that from my relatives."

He stops and opens the case, turning back toward me. He speaks slowly but with little emotion. "I bet you don't often have people tell you things you don't want to hear."

I hate people like this. Superior, condescending.

"That's not necessarily true. You don't even know me. People have influence on others. We can inspire or demoralize. Maybe you need your sense of superiority to keep people away."

He crunches his eyebrows together as if to argue. "Hmm. I hope not . . . You aren't the first to insinuate such a thing." He starts mumbling while he packs up his computer and the projector. "Maybe that's what Claire was talking about."

"Claire?"

"My cousin. I gotta go."

And just like that, he slings a laptop bag over his shoulder and picks up a case and leaves the room.

I've finally met the infamous Kaden. And I hate him.

chapter twelve

I have nothing to wear to school.

As in, nothing.

A massive pile of laundry that I've dumped on the floor all needs to be rewashed. Everything smells like cardboard boxes or plastic bags. What's worse, nothing looks cute or like a style I'd wear at my new school anyway. What is my style now? All-American girl—what is that? And no thank you.

I slump on the floor beside the pile, lifting up a yellow shirt and khaki capris, then a red jacket and a blue dress. Nothing looks good.

My style gravitates around my mood. Some days I wear jeans and a T-shirt or sweatshirt, other days a fun dress with bold accessories and bright shoes, another day maybe all black with heavier makeup. Changing styles is what I'm known for at home. My friend Jeffers would see my outfit du jour and name my mood: *Hello, Energetic. Hello, Happy. Whoa, it's Rebellious. Oh, come here—Miss Melancholy needs a hug.*

"We need to leave in ten minutes," Mom calls from outside my door.

I drop the clothes in frustration as I hear her footsteps hurry down the stairs. With moving and everything, Mom hasn't had time to take me shopping. At home, Carson and I would go to the mall a lot. I could easily get him to take me, and sometimes he'd ask me to go with him. He's a jeans and T-shirt kind of guy, but Carson is very particular about those jeans and shirts and shoes. His friends tease that he's the best-dressed mountain man the wildlife have ever seen. Girls like how he dresses as well.

I wonder what he's been up to. He probably has one of his friends going to the mall with him since I'm not there. Thinking about Carson and the fact that we still haven't connected only increases my aggravated mood—though he left me a lame voice mail—"Hey, don't be mad. I'll visit soon. Sorry though. Bye."

I dig frantically through the clothes, then stop. Why am I doing this? I can't wear these smelly clothes anyway. The closet doesn't offer anything better. My hanging clothes are my adventurous styles, and I'm not ready to stand out like that at school just yet. I hurry out of my room in my pajama bottoms and a T-shirt.

"Mom!" I call down the stairs. "I can't go to school. I have nothing to wear!"

"What? I can't hear you!"

I run down the stairs, the wood floor cold beneath my bare feet.

"I can't go to that school."

"Why not?" she asks as she gets a bowl from the cabinet.

"I just can't."

"Why?'

Mom has no idea that the girls carry purses and backpacks that cost more than my entire outfit or a month's check working at the Underground. That I'm suddenly the poor kid, when at home people asked me where my clothes came from. Suddenly our family is lower class, unintelligent, not at all unique. Even Mom being a magazine writer isn't as interesting in an area teeming with Pulitzer prize winners, movie people, politicians, and everything else imaginable.

"Just forget it." I head back toward the stairs.

"You have to tell me if you want me to understand."

But I don't want to tell her. It'll only make her feel bad. We can't spend all our money so I can compete fashionably with the kids at school.

"I can't find anything to wear," I say and turn away so she doesn't see the tears welling up in my eyes.

"I have your jeans in the dryer if that helps." She quickly pulls out brown sugar, milk, and rice milk and sets them on the counter.

Yeah, my American Eagle jeans. They were cool back home but are like Wal-Mart to these kids. But it's better than what I have, which is nothing. "Fine."

"Fine?"

I know Mom's annoyed that I don't say thank you, but how can I? I mean, really?

"I really don't want to go to school."

"Ruby. Why?"

"I don't want to talk about it." Strangely, I don't know *how* to talk about it. I don't even know why I'm suddenly so upset.

"Okay." She stands at the counter with that confused look she gets when she's trying to figure out how to help me but can't. "Well, if you don't want to talk about it, then why don't you go to school again today. If you absolutely hate it, we'll have to discuss that. And why don't you pray about it?"

"Pray about it?" I say this in my best you've-got-to-be-kidding-me tone. What planet is she on?

But then, this is what I once would've believed. It sort of *is* what I believe. Pray for things that are hard, that make you unhappy, that you don't know what to do about. So why do I feel so contrary now? Maybe because it sounds completely stupid to pray for the fact that I hate school because I'm no longer special or popular or whatever it is that I was in Cottonwood and am not in Marin.

"Sweetie, God can . . ."

But that's all I hear. I nod and look at Mom, but I simply can't process this right now.

"'Kay," I say when she's done. "I'd better hurry and get ready."

She stares at me a moment longer with a strange look. I can't decide if it's worry, disappointment, or sadness. I leave quickly and find a shirt and jacket that are acceptable and get my jeans from the dryer. They're warm as I slide them on. Then I put my books in my crappy book bag that I loved only two months ago.

Why is everything so hard?

Frankie sends me a text between first and second period.

FRANKIE: What's wrong with you today?
ME: How do you know something is wrong?
FRANKIE: I have my ways.

ME: Your ways?

FRANKIE: Never doubt the power of Frankie.

FRANKIE: You walked by the cafeteria with such a sour
look for Little Mary Sunshine.

ME: I couldn't find anything to wear.

FRANKIE: Yeah, I noticed.

FRANKIE: JK, JK. Thought I'd say that before you took me
seriously.

ME: Thanks.

FRANKIE: So our poor girl doesn't have any clothes?

ME: You were nice for three seconds.

FRANKIE: Oh come on now. Want something from me?

ME: Uh, no thanks.

FRANKIE: Girl, I meant from my sister. She just left for
college and put a pile of clothes aside to give away.

I'm not sure how to respond.

FRANKIE: Some are brand-new. She's about your size. I'll
bring you some stuff this afternoon.

"So that was pretty cool."

I'm in world history, and a girl I don't recognize sits on the
desk in front of me.

"Uh, what was pretty cool?"

"You."

The girl is one of those redheads with the perfect fair skin and such natural light in the red of her hair that you want to touch it.

"At the Underground. With Hillary."

And then I remember. The redhead's hair was pulled back when I saw her with the other mean girls. She was the one who wouldn't follow Hillary and her gang.

"Oh, that." What else can I say?

"So you're new here?"

"Yeah."

"I'm London." She reaches out her hand and laughs with the ease of a model, brushing her hair back from her face with manicured fingers.

"I'm Ruby."

"Yes, I know. You're at the top of Hillary's hate list. But don't worry, it's a long list, and someone will most likely replace you by the end of the day. Might have already. I haven't talked to her all weekend."

"So you two are . . . friends?"

"Not really. Our parents are friends. You know how that can be."

She's wearing a loose gray dress with a thick black belt around her thin waist. I can only guess at the brand—Roxy or H&M or . . . Vera Wang. Though I don't really know the very expensive brands of clothing.

"I guess."

"Maybe we could hang out sometime."

I try hiding my surprise, but I don't think I succeed, because she laughs again. "Not with those other girls. It's rare that I'm around them. My closest friends are pretty normal."

"Define 'normal'," I say, and this makes us both laugh.

After class, London comes alongside me as if we're friends. "So, are you seeing anyone?"

"No," I say and think of Nick. "You?"

"I have a huge crush on Anthony Restiva. Do you know him?"

Her voice and movements are so smooth and feminine that I feel awkward just standing there, wondering how I should stand, what looks natural and also feels natural.

"I don't know anyone."

"Come here, quick." She threads her arm through mine and pulls me around the corner that overlooks the main courtyard. "You can't let him see us staring, but Anthony will be walking by in about ten seconds."

"What does he look like?"

"You'll know it's him when you see him. He was my partner in seventh-grade ethnic dance, and I've had a crush on him ever since."

As we lean on the railing over the sea of students who represent every stripe of liberal America, from rockers, revolutionaries, and Greenpeace types to jocks, future fraternity brothers, and tomorrow's CEOs, someone comes up beside me and leans out to see what we're looking at. I try ignoring him, thinking it's Super Jock, but then from the corner of my eye I recognize him.

Kaden.

"Uh, hi?" I say. Dang, this guy is incredibly attractive. He smells great too.

London leans forward to see who it is and smiles widely. "Well, hello, Kaden."

"Hey, London," he says with the same seriousness as usual. Then he says to me, "I was too hard on you the other night. Sorry. Here. Tell your family hello." He hands me a flyer, and before I respond, he walks on, disappearing into the crowd of students.

"Uh," I say.

London is smiling at me. "Nice. And you've been here, what, a week?"

"Who is he anyway?"

"One of the most mysterious guys on campus."

"Why mysterious?"

"A lot of girls have a crush on Kaden. But for all we know, he has a long-distance girlfriend, he's secretly gay, or there's something psychotic about him. Kaden hasn't dated anyone that anyone knows about since he came here last year from somewhere—we don't even know that."

"What else don't you know?"

London squeezes my arm and motions with her head. "There's Anthony, coming from the cafeteria. Blond," she says.

I'm surprised at the guy such a beautiful girl would stare at from afar. He reminds me of a boy band singer, thin, smaller, and pretty average looking.

"Cute," I say, but London is ignoring me as she watches without watching Anthony.

I look at the flyer in my hand. FILM GROUP. THURSDAY NIGHT. 7 P.M. THE UNDERGROUND.

London reads over my shoulder and says, "I think you need to go."

chapter thirteen

Carson is watching TV with his feet on the coffee table and a giant sandwich on a plate resting on his lap. I'm so surprised to see him there that it takes me a moment to believe he's not an illusion. I stand in the doorway and stare.

"Want some?" he asks, pointing to the sandwich.

That's no illusion.

"I ate on the drive down and can't eat all of it."

I open my mouth, but no words come out. What do I say to my brother, watching TV and eating a sandwich? That I'm furious at him for abandoning me?

I *am* angry at him for leaving us—me, Mac, Mom. But I also want to say that I miss him. I don't want to feel angry, don't want to make him guilty. I want us to go do something, maybe drive to the beach Frankie took me to and drink coffee as the sun goes down.

Carson and I have always fought a lot, but sometimes we have more fun with each other than with most anyone else. He's the only one who understands certain things, even if we don't really talk about them. We're not the type of brother and sister to sit and share our feelings. It's enough just to sit beside each other or go somewhere with the music loud. Or to have each other in the same house.

"What?" he asks, all Carson-irritated-like.

"I didn't even see your truck."

"Probably 'cause I had to park blocks down the street."

"I didn't know you were coming."

"I didn't either. But Kate told Allen that you and Mom and Mac were upset that I'm staying with Dad and Tiffany. Oh, and your friendly voice mail."

"You just didn't show up. That was pretty shocking. Suddenly you're living with Dad, after we all thought we'd be together."

"This is a nice warm welcome," he says and leans back on the couch.

I flop down beside him, suddenly angrier than I've been the whole time I've been missing him.

"Wanna go to the mall later?" he asks, and I catch a small smile on the corners of his lips.

This is Carson's apology, and my anger quickly dissipates.

"Well, yeah," I say sarcastically, and then we both smile. "What about tomorrow after I work?"

"Austin and I are going to a Giants preseason thing in the morning." He raises his eyebrows with a smile at that.

"So that's why you came down?"

"No, I came down because I missed you." He grabs my head and starts rubbing it, and I fight him off.

I pick up the other half of his sandwich and take a bite.

"How's Dad?"

"Annoying."

"Why?"

"Long story. He didn't want me to come down, let's just say that."

"How's everyone else up there?"

"Fine, but you better call that little friend of yours."

"Which one? Why?"

"Kate. She likes this senior from another school. It's some big secret."

"Kate hasn't told me about any guy. She liked Derek or Chad last I heard."

"That was days ago. It's all changed in Kate's world. Girls are so weird."

"I'd better call her then."

"Their parents went to some bluegrass festival in Oregon for the weekend. She's staying with that girl you don't like."

"Meegan?"

"Yeah."

"What the heck is going on?"

Meegan is the last person I like Kate around. Then I remember how Kate hasn't really been talking to me. I'd thought it was because I was too busy, that she was angry at me over it.

"Hey, how do you like the new school?" Carson asks with a smirk.

"Yeah, thanks a lot. Deserting me to the likes of Ro-day-o Drive or the OC. I think I saw a girl who was on *My Super Sweet Sixteen*."

"Really?"

"No, but it wouldn't surprise me." I notice he's watching *The Godfather*, and it's paused on the scene when Sonny gets rubbed out.

"You can handle it better than me. Now that you've been there, can you imagine me at that school? Mom told me it's larger than Shasta College."

"It might be. But you might like it. They offer a lot of cool classes. Way more than Cows 101 at home."

"Oh, so you're gonna diss your old school now that you're a big-city girl."

I give him a look and take another bite of sandwich. "Why aren't you in school?"

He smiles. "Oh, I'm exploring colleges in the Bay Area."

"Uh-huh. Well, it's about time you got here. Let's do something fun this weekend."

"Yeah, sure. I should get on the road early Sunday though."

My mouth is full of bread, lettuce, tomato, roast beef, and avocado. It keeps me from commenting on his departure. So this is how it's going to be now?

I nod toward the TV. "Haven't you seen this enough?"

"Never enough, never," he says in a *Godfather* voice. "Mom says there's no satellite TV yet, so I brought a bunch of movies. It'll be classic movie weekend."

"What kind of classics?" I ask and then remember the flyer for the film group tonight.

"*Planet of the Apes, The Birds, Spiderman 1*," he says with a smile.

I pick up a pile of DVDs and hold up *The Shawshank Redemption, Vertigo*, and *Simon Birch*.

Simon Birch. "Did you hear about Little Tony Arnold?"

"Yeah," my brother says solemnly. "Weird. Who'd ever guess? But it made me think of that movie, so I brought it for Mac—I think he's old enough."

"You might cry again if we watch it," I tease, but I know I'll cry if I watch it, just thinking of Little Tony dead and in some coffin at the funeral home. Or maybe he's already in the ground.

"Shut up."

Mom calls from another room, "Don't say 'shut up.'"

We laugh, and it's like normal again. For a few days anyway.

The clothes Frankie drops off aren't the usual hand-me-downs. Quite a few shirts, pants, and jackets still have the tags on them.

"Are you sure about this?" I ask in amazement. Except for a few items, they are exactly what I'd buy if I had the money.

"They would've gone to some charity, so why not to poor little Ruby?"

"I'm not finding that joke funny."

"Oh, but you do. You know you do."

Though he just barely comes in the door—he has an orthodontist appointment, though his teeth look perfect—Frankie says again how he loves our house. As in *loves*, like hyper, exciting, flamboyant loves. He wants the full tour next time—when he was here before, he was more focused on impressing the parents. Carson meets him a bit grudgingly. And then, like a whirlwind that comes and goes, Frankie is gone.

"Who was that?" Carson asks with a frown on his face.

"Frankie," I say cheerily.

"Why are you hanging out with him?"

"I like him. And he brought me clothes."

He's shaking his head. "Don't let being here change you."

"What's that supposed to mean? I would've hung out with Frankie in Cottonwood."

"Dad wouldn't let you."

"Dad lets me do whatever I want."

"Why would you want to hang out with a gay guy?"

"He was the first person to be nice to me. He's my only friend so far." I stand with my hands on my hips, the boxes of clothing on the floor before me.

"Well, nice first friend."

"He's been more fun than half my friends in Cottonwood."

"What's wrong with Cottonwood suddenly?"

"What's your fear about being around a gay guy? He won't make a pass at you."

Carson gets that super-angry quiet that means I've pushed too far.

"I'm going to look at my new clothes."

"Yeah, go do that."

"And by the way, every place we live ends up changing us."

"Whatever."

I know my brother will get over it quickly. He always does. I'll come down in an hour or so and we'll watch movies all night, maybe go to the mall as well.

The clothes, three boxes full, are amazing. I lay them out all over my room. Everything I try on fits me. It's like a fashion miracle.

This could be an answer to prayer, couldn't it? But I didn't end up praying about it after all. Mom might have. Or maybe God hears us without our even asking, reminding us that He's there.

Then why does He seem so far away lately?

My fault?

His fault?

Maybe He's not even there.

But my two most immediate needs are being met—friendship and clothing. Frankie, my new gay friend; London, my apparent friend in the making; and Frankie's boxes of clothing are definite miracles. They do say that God can use anyone and anything.

After a long night of movies, I wake up, and I'm crying. Moonlight streams through the balcony, which is what makes me know I was dreaming—the discovery of which is a relief, like thinking something bad has happened to someone and finding out it's not true. My pillow is damp from the tears.

But the dream wasn't bad or sad, not really.

Pulling the covers up to my chin, I picture the scene that's probably more memory than dream. We were driving in my dad's old Chevy. Mac wasn't born yet, or at least he wasn't there. Dad was driving, Carson and I were in the middle sharing a seat belt, and Mom was on the other side. We were driving somewhere far, because it felt like we'd been on the road forever. We went through a drive-thru and Dad was being goofy to the teller, who was laughing. Carson was saying, "Dad, don't. That's embarrassing." Mom was laughing a little.

And then we had our food, but it wasn't burgers. It was Chinese takeout, but dream-fashion, we're eating with our chopsticks without any trouble at all. And the truck is warm, someone turned on soft music, the night is upon us, and we're driving, going somewhere, anywhere, but going there together. Carson and I are safely tucked between our parents, Mac is a future coming to us, and everything is good and peaceful.

I hate those dreams.

Now it's like my body is afraid of sleep, despite the fact that my mind keeps telling it everything's fine. My body doesn't believe my mind, and so I toss and turn.

Finally I get up and turn on my desk light, then pick up Aunt Betty's gift and hop back beneath the covers. A journal for my thoughts. So why not this one? And so I write.

Maybe it's from all the movies we watched tonight and all the film stuff lately, but I can picture these ideas as scenes in a movie. Maybe it's from Kaden reminding me of that screenwriting workshop. What was it he said that I didn't want to hear? Truth. That sometimes we should stick with something and let it find us.

I write, "Guy sitting on bed with laptop. Night."

The possibilities from there are endless.

Maybe I'll turn it into a horror with something smashing through the window.

Or a romance where he's writing the story of a lost love. Oh, that's sort of like *Moulin Rouge*. It could be a comedy. Hmm, I can't think of anything funny tonight. A bucket of water falls on his head. No, that's about as funny as a sad dream.

A suspense film could have a stranger pop on with an IM

threatening the guy's secret love. How does the stranger know he's in love with her?

Or the phone could ring—it's a woman, crying out for help.

I snuggle down in my covers and release a long, open-mouthed yawn. And as the ideas come one after another, I write and think and travel toward sleep with the images surrounding me.

chapter fourteen

"We're here to pick you up, but we want milkshakes!" Mac says as he races into the Underground with Carson following.

"It's only three o'clock. I'm not off for another half hour."

Carson smiles one of his happier smiles. He must have enjoyed the Giants today. "That's why we came for milkshakes. And so I could see Aunt Jenna," he says just as I hear a cry of excitement from the kitchen.

Aunt Jenna races toward Carson and envelops my brother in a big hug.

I make chocolate milkshakes, and Aunt Jenna tells me to have one with them. It's a slow time, so she visits for a while, then leaves us to drink our milkshakes and let Mac tell jokes.

"There were these three fifth graders in an airplane . . ."

Sometimes it's easy not to actually listen to Mac, since he talks continuously.

"Do you get it?"

We're silent a moment, and then Carson laughs, which makes

me laugh, which always happens when Carson laughs. It makes me happy to see him happy, though I don't know why this is.

"You get it?" Mac keeps saying.

This is how it would be. This would be normal if Carson still lived with us.

But I'm trying not to let *what if* and *if only* and *would be* take over what *is*. This is something Natasha said to me earlier today. I told her that my brother was visiting and that I wished he wouldn't go back.

She nodded, and I could tell she had something to say, so I asked her. With a divorce and a second husband's death behind her, she said that she can't live in what might have been or what would be.

"I missed a lot of years wishing my life were something else. Now I try to take the gift of today and as many tomorrows as are given to me and do all I can in that time."

If I were to write what I've been given today, chocolate milk-shakes with my brothers would be the first thing I'd put down.

In the evening we work on the house, unpacking and cleaning. Carson works on his apartment, for when he comes down to visit or when other company comes. He talks about bringing some of his friends to go deep-sea fishing or sailing with a friend of Austin's.

Then we go out for late-night Chinese, and I think of my dream from last night.

"You didn't really tell me what's going on with Dad," I say to Carson, realizing that I haven't talked to my father in over a week.

"Later," he says, glancing at Mom.

A feeling of longing comes over me, and then I try instead

to enjoy this right now. A time with Mom, Austin, Mac, Carson, and me—it's rare. And who knows, a few years from now, I might dream about this and miss it terribly.

But I will call my dad tonight too.

"I don't want to get up," I tell Mac when he announces that breakfast is ready. The day awakens with a dread like the fog lingering around the house.

"Mom is cooking bacon, eggs, hash browns, and French toast with coconut syrup." He licks his lips. "It's our last breakfast with Carson for a long, long time."

A shadow of sadness washes over Mac's young face. His hair is messy, and he's in pajamas that only little kids should wear—Carson will no doubt tease that Mac is too old for the tight blue-with-yellow-moons top and bottoms. I forget how skinny Mac's legs are, little-kid skinny, and it makes him look like a cute big-headed grasshopper.

"So come down, 'kay?"

"'Kay," I say, but I pull the covers over my head.

At breakfast Austin announces, holding a bite of French toast midair on his fork, "Let's go to the beach."

"But Carson has to leave soon," Mom says.

"No, I can stay longer. It's no big deal."

This brightens everyone up.

An hour later we're at the beach instead of church. I must admit, I was actually looking forward to church, to "trying out" the one Kaden attends. But Carson says he won't be back for a month, so this is better. Mom packs a ton of food, and after breakfast and Chinese, I wonder if I'll fit into those new clothes of mine tomorrow.

Above the silver waters the fog lingers, but it's not too cold, and the sky is slowly fading from gray into patches of blue. The waves come in a steady rhythm to roll and fold, then stretch themselves across the sand. Mac and Carson play catch with a Nerf football. Austin tries to fly a kite but finally gives up. Mom gets up from the sand castle she was making and brushes the sand off her jeans. They walk hand in hand down the beach toward some craggy rocks.

After all the food I've been eating, I should play football or go for a run or something, but this heaviness keeps me resting on the blanket. Running my fingers through the sand, I sift through the cool top layer to the cold underneath, making parallel lines like a Japanese garden.

Usually I'd draw pictures in the sand or wishes or the name of my current crush. *Ruby loves* . . .

I think of Nick. But I don't love Nick. I don't even really like him. I haven't thought of him, wondered about him, or talked to him in days.

When I was thirteen, I thought I loved a guy who worked at my dad's hardware store. And there have been some strong emotions for Chad Michael Murray and Orlando Bloom, as well as real-life crushes on a few guys at school, which were usually reciprocated. Those ended for various reasons.

But right now I wouldn't write *Ruby loves* or even *Ruby likes* about anyone.

Dad wasn't home when I called the night before. The

answering machine said, "You've reached the home of Steve and Tiffany Madden," which conjured a strange anger. There was no mention of "Carson, Ruby, or Mac." Though it isn't my home. But it is my dad's.

And Carson lives there. Carson and my dad.

And me, Mac, and Mom live together with Austin. I should be thankful for this, for today. But somehow I can't be.

A sadness prevails like the fog prevailing over the sunny day, even if the sky promises to turn blue once again. Not long ago I was at this same ocean with Frankie, and the world stretched before me all hopeful and wonderful-like.

The waves roll and stretch, roll and stretch, as they do with faithful eternal consistency.

All I feel now is a great sense of looming unrest. What will become of us all?

ME: We need to talk soon, but I can't right now. Carson
    is about to leave.
KATE: It's like we're becoming strangers, and we always
    promised to be BFF.
ME: I know. So let's talk tonight.
KATE: K. L8r G8r

Carson and I carry his bag and a few boxes out to his truck and then stand outside in the falling darkness. He was supposed to leave in the morning, but he keeps delaying.

"I can't believe we won't ever live together anymore," I say, no longer caring if that hurts his feelings.

"Yeah."

"I'm not trying to make you feel bad."

"Uh-huh."

"How often will you come down?"

"I don't know."

We hear Mac's voice inside the house. "I'll give him my room." Mom's voice is muffled, so we can't hear what she says—only Mac then responds, "So I'm not even going to see him anymore! When I see Dad, Carson'll probably be here seeing you. I hate this!"

"It's the meltdown," I say, though Mac has appropriately expressed my pent-up emotions.

"Poor guy. I need to do more with him when we're together." Carson opens the tailgate of his truck with a creak. "But I don't belong here. I mean, my truck uses more gas in a week than some of these cars use in a month."

"You could get a hybrid." I'm only half joking.

"There aren't many electrical plugs in the Trinity Alps. Though the new ethanol trucks might be an option." He sits on the tailgate. In the back of his truck are some boxes, his sleeping bag, a fishing pole, tackle box, and a container full of camping supplies.

He doesn't really fit down here, it's true. And yet . . .

"There are tons of things for you to do," I say. "People in Marin are really into the outdoors. They cycle everywhere, hike Mount Tamalpais, sea kayak, go on ecotours."

"It's yuppie adventures. I like going where I don't see a soul for a whole day. Where there are thousands of acres separating me from civilization. Sometimes I can't think with people pressing in."

This is a lot for Carson to verbalize. He's been thinking this over, I can tell.

"And besides," he says, "Dad needs me."

"Why does Dad need you?" This worries me. Dad *needing* Carson—is something wrong with him? Does he need me too?

"I can't really explain it."

"What about Mom?"

"She misses me, and I miss her. I miss her more than I ever expected. But Dad—it's just different. Like he's unhappy without us. It's tiring in a way. You know, Dad got remarried fast for a reason."

"What do you mean?"

I'm not getting this at all. It's true Dad married only months after the divorce. We hated it, hated him sometimes, and hated them both for all the changes. And then Mom started telling us about Austin, and one night Carson and I planned to run away with Mac. Carson wanted to go to Alaska, and I wanted to go to New York or Paris. We got in a fight and went to our rooms instead.

"Men have a hard time being alone."

"That's what Mom said when Dad got married."

"I guess for a lot of men, it's true. Not me. I love being alone sometimes. But Tiffany works those twelve-hour shifts at the hospital, so I usually do something with him those nights. He's pretty lonely when she's working, and he's not the same without his kids. It's not really fair for Mom to get all of us."

"It's not really fair that they got a divorce." I sit on the tail-gate, and my feet dangle off the edge.

Carson shouldn't have such responsibility, and yet the idea of

Dad sitting at his house alone is pretty disturbing. I think about Dad's friends and family up there. Why doesn't he do things with them? Before I ask, we hear Mac crying from inside the house.

"I'm going with him!"

"Remember when Mac disappeared, and Mom and Dad thought he was kidnapped?"

We laugh at the memory, even though it wasn't funny at the time. After about a half hour of searching and Mom calling 911, Carson carried in a sheepish Mac.

"For some reason, I just knew he was under my bed," Carson says with a laugh. "Mac said he was scared he'd be in trouble for hiding, so he didn't want to come out."

"He's always doing things we never would have done."

"Yeah, remember when he almost got hit by that car?"

We get quiet at that memory. There's no humor in it. We saw both Mom and Dad cry that day. And sometimes I find it terribly sad that two people could love each other so much, see a miracle occur with their child, and then eventually break up.

"He shouldn't have lived through it."

"Yeah," Carson says solemnly.

"You know, just because they couldn't stay together, we can't . . ."

"Yeah, but what do we do?"

Weird how my brother understands what I'm saying. We're so different, like *so* different. And yet some things can't be understood by anyone else in the world.

"We'd better get in for dinner." Carson hops off the tailgate.

"Yeah, the last supper."

"Will the guilt ever end?"

"Sorry."

And we both smile.

"Listen here, little sister, I'm just trying it out. I mean, the truth is, neither house is ideal. If I stay here, I don't belong among the rich and ultra-educated."

"And there?"

"Where is home now? Tell me. Is it here? Or is it back in the town we lived in all our lives? In another year I'll get a house of my own or go to college, maybe even down here. I'm adaptable. It just takes me a little longer."

A half hour later Carson and I finish eating a piece of Mom's cheesecake. Mom rarely makes dessert, and I wonder if it's an attempt to keep Carson longer. Mac and Austin are playing Legos in Mac's room, so there's no dramatic departure.

"So call and tell me you made it. There shouldn't be much traffic. You know how to get to the San Rafael Bridge, right?"

Mom has that fake everything-is-okay tone in her voice, not wanting to make Carson feel guilty but unable to really succeed. I guess that's what love is though. Someone always gets pain of one kind or another, even if that pain is the love itself.

All the terrible good-bye stuff, kisses, I love yous. Carson nods at me, and I give my unemotional good-bye. My heart feels frozen in my chest, and I know he doesn't want any more displays of affection.

But when I hear his truck door slam, something in my heart drops. Then the roar of his engine, and I run for the door. He's staring at the house, not pulling out yet.

I put up my hand as if to stop him, and he rolls down his window.

"Did I forget something?"

"No," I say with a shake of my head. Why does it feel like he's going off to war or leaving for a year in outer space instead of going back to Cottonwood? Maybe because life is changing around me so fast, and it feels I should just hang on tight and see where it takes me. "Tell Dad that I love him."

"You tell him yourself. See you soon," he calls and then backs out the driveway and is gone.

How long I stand there, I don't know. I don't know anything anymore. My brother will be crossing the San Rafael Bridge now. My dad is probably happy that one of his children will be up there full-time. I don't know where Mom went, but it certainly wasn't to the movies like she said—Austin didn't even go with her. And I'm standing outside in the cold late evening waiting for something to happen, to feel better, for life to miraculously be good, for God to come tell me it's okay, for my brother to come back and say he's only kidding.

I walk to the road and sit down, right there on the curb.

Time is passing around me. I don't really hear the footsteps, and yet some part of my brain does hear because it isn't a surprise to feel a presence beside me. I want to tell him to go away, that I need a moment alone. He's been driving me crazy off and on all week, and I sort of want to tell him that too. But I'm too tired to say it. The words feel too heavy to form in my mouth. And it's strangely nice having him silent beside me. If he talks though . . .

"Are you okay, Rubes?" Mac asks.

I don't respond. If I do, I might say words I regret, and then the annoying, adorable little guy will be hurt. There's enough hurt sitting here beside us on the curb, I decide.

"I understand," he says with a nod in that funny adult voice he sometimes uses. It nearly makes me smile.

We sit together on the curb. A few cars pass, and then we see that guy with the weird solar unicycle. Mac looks at me with a surprised expression that he must see reflected on my face. It makes us laugh for a moment, and the guy keeps going, silhouetted against the streetlamps, his shadow looking like a strange flamingo on wheels.

The silence comes again. The silence of night and distant cars, someone's lawn sprinklers, and voices far away. The kind of silence that rests between two people, even if they are fifteen and ten. It's the silence that can feel awkward or like a warm blanket against the cold.

I feel Mac's hand touch mine. I open my hand, and his soft little fingers rest curled in my palm. We don't look at each other, only at the night and the street before us. And I guess it's such gestures and moments that make the world still beautiful and the night at peace.

chapter fifteen

"We're a group of students exploring and developing our artistic nature through the medium of filmmaking," Rob, the leader of the film group, tells me. It's only the two of us so far, and I fidget in my chair uncomfortably.

This is brave for me—coming even to a familiar location like the Underground—to join a group that I know nothing about. I don't do things like this. Without London, Frankie, and Kate pushing me to try it, I probably would've stayed home, especially knowing the dreaded Blair is part of this group. Frankie isn't though; he's taking a hiatus from film since the last Premiere Night. That Kaden might be here may have stirred some of my courage as well. I haven't seen him at school at all since he gave me the flyer.

I came a few minutes early, and boy, am I regretting that. Rob and I are sitting at one of the long tables that reminds me of a medieval banquet hall. Two employees I hadn't met before work the counter, though I made my own vanilla almond tea with cream and sugar after introducing myself.

But this is one of those times I should have been late, sitting behind everyone else and listening like an eavesdropper as I decide if this is something I want to join or not. Instead I have to make small talk with Rob. He's a senior at Marin High and sort of cute, but not at all my type. Though I don't quite know what *is* my type.

"Do you have experience in making movies?" he asks.

"None whatsoever."

"Ah, brand-new. That's refreshing."

"Refreshing? I thought that might make it harder."

"It can be refreshing in that you aren't showing up ready to take over. We've had a few people with years of experience, which is both an asset and a challenge. Some people have left because we couldn't agree on work ethic, projects, and visions."

I sip my tea and pour in another packet of natural sugar. "So how long have you been involved in film?"

"I made my first film when I was three years old, with a bit of help from my father."

"Guess I'm coming to this late in life," I joke, but wonder if it's true. It doesn't seem right that filmmaking should be like, say, ice skating or tennis, where once you hit your twenties, you're too late. "I'm sure there are plenty of people who don't start until they're much older."

"I guess some. It's just what I've always loved. My dad is a producer."

"You mean like a movie producer?"

"Yeah. He's produced a lot of indie type movies and is now doing some major films. He's in Morocco right now coproducing a film that has Pacino in it. Frank Darabont is directing."

"Cool," I say, though I don't know who Frank Darabont is, and I only know Pacino because he's my stepdad's favorite actor. These people may be way beyond me, and this is reaffirmed as they start arriving.

A guy wearing all black right down to his cowboy boots is introduced as Darren Duke. Darren introduces Cass, who's dressed in a perfect rendition of the fifties, with cute horn-rimmed glasses, a plaid dress, and thick pumps. Next arrive brothers Josef, with the *J* pronounced like a *Y*, and Vladamir; then another guy called Sound Guy, or SG; and Olivia, who is obviously one of the actresses in the group.

Still no sign of Kaden. *This isn't a date,* I remind myself. He handed me the flyer and didn't wait to see if I was interested. Maybe he doesn't even attend.

Rob finds it necessary to introduce me, including that I'm new to the area, which starts a Q&A session that I'd rather avoid.

"Where did you say you're from?"

"What school do you go to here?"

"I would die in one of those small towns."

"I thought you looked familiar. How many days a week do you work here?"

"Hey, could I get a Parisian café?" asks Sound Guy, nudging my arm.

I stare at him for a moment, but before I respond, he says, "Rob said you work here."

"Yeah, I do." But I can't figure out if he's joking or not.

"Great. I'd like extra whip on that." He smiles widely and waits.

"It's her day off," a voice says, and a foot kicks the guy's chair from behind.

I turn in my seat to see Kaden taking a seat behind us.

Sound Guy laughs. "Just wondered if I could make her do it anyway."

Before anyone says more, Rob brings the group back to the topic. "Okay, let's get started. We're missing Blair, but we'll proceed."

"Blair has arrived," someone says, and she certainly has.

She walks up with confidence and pride and a frown on her face. She's Queen Elizabeth I in Vera Wang.

"Don't let me keep you from proceeding." She pulls a chair up beside me, and the scent of expensive perfume follows as she leans close to me and whispers, "So you're interested in making Christian films to spread the gospel?"

Rob speaks before I can respond. "This month we're going to watch the movies directed by Tony Scott, and then if you want a jump start on next month, we'll be checking out the work of his brother, Ridley Scott."

"So *Top Gun* and *Gladiator*," Darren Duke says.

Cass says dramatically, "Two months of watching action flicks. Wonderful."

"You'll be surprised at some of their lesser-known films," Rob says with confidence. He hands out papers with a list of films that Tony Scott directed and a short bio about his life.

Blair leans near me and whispers, "You might not be able to watch some of those films. I think they're rated R."

"We have two months before the final Premiere Night of this school year, and since a few of us will be graduating right after—

including me—this will truly be my final one. So let's break into our groups. We'll come back together to talk about last month's theme—Alfred Hitchcock's early works."

Two groups form, and I wait, glancing around in time to see Kaden going back outside.

Rob turns a chair backward and sits down. "I have some introductory papers if you want to read them. Our meetings vary. The first one of the month—this one—is usually more business at first, then we discuss a movie or a director. We get into our groups for a while. The two groups often work on two different films. But now we're working together on a few projects, and we'll perfect one for the end-of-school-year premiere." He hands me a packet of papers. "At the end of the summer, we hope to present a longer film at Film in the Park."

"Sounds amazing."

Rob leaves me to read over the papers.

Soon the group comes back together to discuss the production of their own films. Sitting within the dialogue that even Blair gets into, I'm drawn to what they are saying, fascinated by the idea that they are actually making their own films from beginning to end. These aren't YouTube amateurs; this group takes their work seriously.

My heart actually beats faster as my nervousness disappears, though I'm the outsider. But it's as if someone throws cold water in my face, that's how strong the realization is . . . I want this. I want to take those ideas I worked on the other night and see them come to life. All the times I've dissected movies, the way I imagine and visualize things, the hard work and teamwork it takes to create something . . . so many things come together as I listen in.

I forget Marin and Cottonwood and all the sadness and weirdness, leaning in to take in the buzz of words and energy within the group. And the puzzle piece finally fits. I fit. I've opened a door and found a whole world waiting for me.

The group moves on to discussing *Rebecca*, one of Alfred Hitchcock's films from the novel by Daphne du Maurier. I haven't seen it, but I make notes and decide to get it online as soon as possible. And before I want the meeting to end, people start leaving.

"So what did you think of our little group?" Rob asks.

I want to say that this is exactly what I've been searching for—it's always been in me; I just didn't know it yet. But I want to act nonchalant, not overly emotional. So I nod my head. "Yes. It's . . . really great." I can't withhold a smile.

Rob smiles back. "I saw you taking notes. That's a good indicator. If you want to join, we'll get you into a group and you can jump right in."

"Yes, I'd love that." *Especially if it's with Kaden's group,* I find myself thinking. *He's strange, but interesting. And, yeah, very cute.* "Though I don't know anything."

"At first they'll have you doing the jobs they don't want, but as you learn, you'll get more into the actual production. So next week I'll assign you to a group."

I'm more afraid and more excited than I've felt in a long, long, long, long time. As in, a long time. Maybe since, well, I don't even know when.

Kaden came back when I didn't notice. I see him talking with Sound Guy. As I head toward the front door to see if Austin has arrived to pick me up, Kaden's voice stops me.

"Something that helped me was watching movies in themes. Like the top hundred best films, or the best films of 1960. It's surprising how much you start understanding when you do that."

"Sounds like good advice."

"What's your favorite movie?"

"*The Passion of the Christ?*" Blair asks sarcastically as she walks by.

"Probably *The Princess Bride*," I say, and Blair gives a backwards smirk.

Sound Guy says, "I love that movie! 'No more rhymes, now I mean it!'"

"'Anybody want a peanut?'" I say, along with several others in the group.

Kaden's eyes are the darkest brown, nearly black, and framed by lashes so dark it looks like natural eyeliner. There is an intensity in his gaze that makes me unable to think of any other movies.

Sound Guy tells Kaden and me good-bye and heads to the door still quoting. "'To the pain!' 'Inconceivable!' 'I admit it, you are better than I am. Then why are you smiling? Because I know something you don't know.'"

"Did you notice I was friendly this time?" Kaden asks.

I remember that a week ago, I tried hating this guy. Part of me thinks I should try at least disliking him as my heart and head say, *Danger, this one could be dangerous to us.* He has a slight smile on the edges of his lips, lips that are, well, just perfect. *Danger!*

"Oh, is this you being friendly?" I ignore my heart and my head, which is scary because they hardly ever agree with each other.

"Ouch, that's painful," he says with his hand covering his

heart, and then we both laugh. "If you want, I'll give you my list of the top hundred best films."

"Sure, I'll give you my e-mail." And I can't keep away my smile the entire time I write it out and hand it to him.

He looks at his watch. "Oh, crap. I gotta run. I'll write you soon."

"Bye, Kaden," Blair says, coming up beside me as I watch him go.

But not even Blair can dampen one of the most amazing and perhaps life-altering nights of my life so far.

Austin picks me up and wants to hear about school, the group, and everything, though I'm having a hard time talking about it until I process it more in my head. And as we pull into the drive-way, the house, when it comes into view, feels like it really is my house.

We walk inside, and the smell of fajitas makes my mouth water.

Mac pops his head out and says, "I made brownies."

Mom appears, holding a plate of Spanish rice, and tells me to get washed up.

"It's after nine o'clock," I say.

"Which is a normal time for dinner in many places around the world," Mom says. "We've been waiting for you so we can eat together. Austin's dinner inspired me."

And I smile at that because my family, even without Carson here, feels like my family. I hurry upstairs to drop off my bag and wash my hands in my little bathroom, and my room feels like my room.

"Your dad called you back," Mom says. "And Kate called too."

I didn't realize my phone was on mute through the meeting and drive home.

"Call them back after dinner though."

We sit in the living room this time. Austin recorded *Heroes*—I'd forgotten it was on tonight—which is our favorite family TV series, and even Mac is allowed to stay up late for it. It's a rerun tonight, but still we gather around to watch. During commercials, Austin starts reciting what he'd put on a list of top one hundred movies.

"*The Good, the Bad, and the Ugly*; *Unforgiven*; and *The Godfather*."

"*Finding Nemo*," Mac says. He still loves that movie and watches it at least once a month.

The noise of conversation and the TV playing loudly surprises me like a quick jolt, reminding me of a time before, back when Dad would be my dad, the house would be in Cottonwood, Carson would be here, and we'd all be younger. The flashback is so vivid it stuns me. But I brush it away, watching it fade the way movies make the transformation from a historical event to the modern time.

Everything keeps changing. Time isn't slowing down for me to figure everything out . . . or even much of anything out. But it's exciting too, these unexpected doors opening up, showing me more of myself and a clearer vision of what I've sensed for so long.

I keep thinking about the film group. And I think of Kaden. I don't even know him. But even though my heart and head are still saying, *Beware, danger ahead,* they have no intention of running away.

chapter sixteen

Kate is coming. Kate is coming.

It's all we talk about when we have time to talk over the next week. I still know very little about her new boyfriend, other than that he's "hot" and it's a huge secret. Kate hasn't told me why it's such a secret or what high school he attends.

"I'll tell you everything when I get there."

With homework, the Underground, and film group, I'm not online as much, and I've noticed a rapid decrease of texts from my friends in Cottonwood. It bothers me, and yet it doesn't bother me since I'm busy enough to keep it from my thoughts. Frankie and I talk often. If Blair weren't also his friend, he'd be the perfect girlfriend. Mom doesn't find the humor in my saying that.

Kaden isn't at film group for two weeks in a row, and I'm not brave enough to ask about him. Once I saw him from a distance at school, and though we tried out the church he attends, he wasn't there either. He never e-mailed me. I checked regularly until my anxiousness turned to anxiety and then to that post-jilted anger.

We tried to warn you, my heart and head tell me. I tell myself that he's not that cute, and that he's strange anyway. Definitely not boyfriend or bridge-guy material.

My film team meets on Friday nights in addition to the usual Thursdays. I was assigned to the team that Blair isn't on, but it doesn't appear that Kaden is part of it either, since no one mentions his absence. Rob is our team leader.

There's a lot to do, he tells me. I take notes to remember everything.

Each team produces a film, and my team is partway through production. Of the two, one is chosen for the competition at the final Premiere Night of the school year. Everyone is getting stressed, and now my team has me—the ultra-novice. I get the script, and Rob explains that for now I'll be the gopher . . . meaning I run errands or do whatever they need me to do. It's starting at the bottom, but I don't mind. Then he gives me a production schedule. We start shooting the same weekend Kate is coming.

Her response to this: "Sounds like fun, maybe they'll want me as an extra."

London now texts regularly, and she treated me to a few hours at her spa. We sat in some kind of herbal bath and then got pedicures. That's a life I could get used to.

The days go on like this until with surprising speed it's the day of Kate's arrival. And I realize, with much guilt, that I don't really want her to come this weekend. I'm not ready to have her hang out with me and the film team. How do I blend Kate and the old life with what's developing but not yet solid in this new life?

I have to work for a few hours after school on Friday. My favorite old guys are there, and I take extra effort to check on their drinks.

I'm organizing the small front refrigerators when I hear my name called. And there's Kate standing at the counter, her smile so wide and adorable that I half expect a little *ding* sound and flash of light from her teeth. She's cut her brown hair shorter than I've seen it. The front curls in at her chin.

Kate.

"Oh my gosh, don't cry on me," she says as I hurry over to embrace her.

"I didn't realize I missed you so much."

Seeing her is like hot cocoa after sledding, a hot bath after running in the rain, a campfire on a camping trip.

"Well, it's about time you started missing me."

"Oh, but I miss you every day," I say and know it's the truth. Then I notice Kate's mom and hug her too.

"Are you off work now? Ready to show us the town?"

"I was just waiting for you."

"It doesn't feel like Aunt Betty's house anymore." Kate flops her duffel bag on my bed and looks around the room.

"I know."

"It's totally you and your mom's kind of place."

"Yeah, I guess it is. It feels like Europe or some little house in a foreign country, huh?"

"Or at least what we think those places would feel like." Kate laughs at that.

"So what do you want to do?" I ask.

"What do you want to do?"

"I made a list of things."

"Cool," she says, glancing around for a place to sit.

"We need a new spot for you."

At the two houses I've lived in since we were kids, we've always had a "Kate's spot" in my room. In our last house, I had her sit in the beanbag against the wall and drew an outline of her. Then we painted and colored a Kate-on-the-beanbag mural in the spot, and so she'd sit there—the two Kates—whenever she came over. We had to paint over it when we moved out.

"Yeah."

"What's wrong?" I ask, and yet I know. What's with the awkwardness?

"Nothing," she says with a touch of sadness hiding in her tone.

"So what's up with this older guy?"

"He's in college."

My mouth drops—I'm sort of bad about letting that happen instead of hiding my shock. "I thought he was a senior at a Redding school."

"That's what most everyone believes."

"No way."

"Yeah," she says with a giggle.

"So what's happening with you and him?" I have to keep my

voice from sounding like my mom's, which surprises me. Am I jealous, or sad that I don't know these things already, or what the heck is wrong with me suddenly?

"Not much, yet," she says with a sly smile. "Wanna see some pics of him?"

And we're back. Whew, that was close.

The film team is meeting at a Vietnamese restaurant. A nervous feeling comes over me as we arrive and I introduce Kate.

Kate tries making everyone laugh and sounds too loud. Or hyper. Or immature. Something that annoys me.

I don't want to be annoyed by her. And suddenly I don't want her to meet any more of my new friends.

"I've never eaten Vietnamese," she says with all the excitement of a kid having her first ice cream. "What's Upseelongobee?" Then she laughs.

It's at this moment I see the stark contrast between Kate and the members of the film team. Kate appears years younger and childlike, or maybe childish. I wouldn't have thought it, not ever.

Cass sits on the other side of Kate, wearing her vintage clothing, leaning back in her chair, and sipping her cup of tea.

Kate doesn't even try adapting or hiding her lack of culture. It's like she shouts out her ignorance with her actions and comments like "So where is Vietnam exactly? I mean, does anyone actually know, other than it's near Japan or China?"

Cass and Sound Guy glance at each other. I want to hide under the table.

Olivia sits down and continues talking to me, though I wasn't really paying attention because I was so worried about Kate. "We'll go to the film festival in the fall. They have one here in Mill Valley. Every year they have directors and actors attend. It's mainly indie films, but some bigger talent is present as well."

And then Kate starts asking a hundred and one questions. "So you actually enter real film festivals? Do you need more actresses?" This is said with a raise of her eyebrows. She then asks about what to order from the waitress and those around us, telling a story about trying Indian food and how that was a big mistake. "I think I spent two days in the bathroom, if you know what I mean."

When she launches into stories from our childhood, approaching the one when we went toilet-papering one of our teacher's houses, I lean toward her and say, "Let's go to the bathroom."

"I don't have to go."

"Yeah, you do."

This gets a snicker out of someone at the table, and Kate looks confused.

Once we're inside, I hiss in frustration, "Kate!" I want to shake her.

"What?" She is completely unaware of how she's looking to the film team. Can't she see how, well . . . how Cottonwood she's acting?

"We're trying to have our meeting."

"What are you talking about?"

"This is supposed to be a working meeting, not just a social time."

"Well, sorry. I was just trying to get to know your friends."

"They aren't really my friends yet."

"So I'm making a bad impression, is that what you're telling me?"

"No." *Yes! You're acting like . . . well, yourself, but like you would with friends you've known forever. Don't you know that when you meet people, you don't . . .*

Nothing sounds right in my own head, so how can I explain it to Kate?

"I'm sorry, never mind. Let's just go back. I guess what I meant was, it's just we need to get to the work part of the meeting. I don't want to be here very long—we need to go have our fun weekend." But I know my voice isn't very convincing.

"Okay," she says quietly. And quiet she is for the rest of the meeting.

I can't concentrate either, glancing toward Kate off and on. They assign me to be at the set on Sunday and give me a list of things to pick up and directions to the site. Other than that, I'm not part of the meeting. We call Mom to pick us up.

Back at home, a tiredness comes over me, but we only have tonight and tomorrow together.

"Unless you really want to see that movie, we could just stay here," Kate suggests. She hasn't said much since the restaurant. "We could watch a movie and get online. I miss James."

I'd forgotten about James—the guy I know nothing about except that he's way too old for my friend. Tonight further emphasized that fact.

"I'll see if Mom will make some brownies, and we can stay in. There's a Hitchcock film I've been wanting to watch."

"Gee, that sounds exciting," she says in a dull voice.

A phone beeps, and we both search our purses.

"Oh, it's Frankie," I say when I find my phone.

"Oh, I want to meet him. But don't worry, I won't talk much."

"Kate—I didn't mean it like that." How did I become the bad guy?

> FRANKIE: Hey, it's Friday night. A bunch of us are going
> into the city. How bout it?

"Tell him to come over. Or come pick us up to do something."

> ME: Oh, I can't. Out-of-town relatives are here.
> FRANKIE: Ugh, hate those.
> ME: Huh?
> FRANKIE: Huh again eh? Anyone who lives out of this
> town is usually BORING!
> ME: Have fun.
> FRANKIE: Yeah, you too girl.

"He can't come over. He's going into the city with a bunch of people." I can't believe all the lies I'm suddenly flinging around. To my Marin best friend, as well as to my best friend of my whole life.

Kate is quiet for a moment. "So he invited you to go too?"

"Uh, yeah, sort of. But I thought we'd have more fun without being around a bunch of strangers. Plus, I have no idea what they're doing—for all I know, they're going gay bar hopping."

"Or you're worried that I'd embarrass you again."

"What? You didn't embarrass me."

She stares at me in that way that makes me squirm. "You can't lie to me. I see right through you."

"It's not like that, Kate. It's just, I still don't really fit here with—"

"What are you talking about? You look totally comfortable with everyone."

"Well, you should know that means nothing. I can act like everything is cool when nothing is at all."

"Yeah, but just because I talk too much when I'm nervous, you could be more supportive. More protective even. You made me feel like an idiot."

"You wouldn't stop talking. That group meets to work, to get things accomplished, not hear stories of us rafting down the creek on a giant piece of Styrofoam or toilet-papering people's houses. You made us sound like country bumpkins."

"They liked my stories."

"No, they didn't."

"Maybe I shouldn't have come." Kate stands up with her arms crossed, glaring at me.

"Maybe you shouldn't have." *How can she really blame this on me?*

She takes a step closer. "You've been down here less than a month—and you've changed."

"No, I haven't."

"Oh yes, you have."

"I think it's you who changed."

"Whatever. You with your film club and new job and elite

school—yeah, it's me who's changed. You have an entirely new life."

"You're secretly dating a guy in college. Oh, that's smart."

"Yeah, I thought it was pretty smart."

"You won't think so when you get a disease or get pregnant."

"Yeah, because I'm sure I'll have sex just because I like an older guy."

"You've never been very smart when it comes to guys."

"You've never thought I was very smart anyway. So why would I be smart with guys?"

"I've never said that."

"You haven't had to. And by the way, I'm glad you're now an expert with men. You've had so many relationships. Which one of us is even dating? I don't see your mature friends, or you for that matter, dating a guy in college."

"And what kind of college guy dates a sophomore in high school?"

We don't talk the rest of the night. Kate ends up playing Clue with Mac. He wants me to play too and offers me Miss Scarlet if I will. I tell him I don't feel good. Then I turn off my phone and go to bed. Kate comes in later and uses my laptop to talk half the night to her college-aged boyfriend. I can only imagine what she's telling him.

The next morning Mom makes French toast and brings it to us in bed. And I wonder, with all her cooking lately, if Mom thinks food is the answer to the world's problems.

"Is this your coconut syrup?" Kate asks sheepishly.

"Yes, it is." Mom smiles.

"Remember when we first tried coconut syrup at that little place in Maui?"

Mom sits on the edge of my bed. "It was the morning before my wedding. I ate so much I worried I wouldn't fit into my dress. But when we got home, I knew French toast would never be the same without coconut syrup."

"That was one of the best trips of my life," Kate says.

And the memories come even after Mom leaves. Snorkeling together until Kate almost drowned when she met a sea turtle eye-to-snorkel mask, screamed, and sucked in a mouthful of water. Surfing lessons, and us so proud that we both got up. We thought about staying in Maui to become full-time surf bums after that.

The wedding was a casual event on the beach, and I was happy to see Mom so happy. I was maid of honor, and Kate did the guest book. Those ten days in Maui were the best trip for best friends.

"I'm sorry," I say between bites of French toast.

"I'm sorry too."

We look at each other, smile, and then we laugh. Maybe food *is* the answer to the world's problems.

And we're back. Again.

We spend the rest of the day shopping in the little boutiques and at the mall. Mom takes us to Sausalito to browse their waterfront and to eat fish and chips at a fun little restaurant overlooking the bay. We make plans to go into the city next time Kate's down.

Sunday morning is good-bye—her mom wants to get home before dark. We hug, and I wave until she's out of sight. There's a moment that she looks sad, and I wonder what's really going on with her. We barely talked about anything of substance after our fight. Does she feel that I've abandoned her? Are we drifting apart so quickly?

We're back, I remind myself as I walk up the stairs to my room. I need a nap, and I'm relieved the taping today is canceled. Something about not enough fog.

> ME TO KATE: It'll be better next time.
> KATE: Yeah, I know.
> ME: We'll go into the city or check out the universities.
> KATE: Yeah, we need to keep making plans for that. If we
>   have money we'll stay in the dorms. Otherwise, it's
>   the garage apartment.
> ME: Exactly.

Will we ever see these plans come true? We've been friends since Mrs. K.'s class in kindergarten.

But can such friendships really last forever?

chapter seventeen

LONDON: What are you doing tonight?
ME: Nada.

I'm cleaning my room on another Friday night and was just thinking maybe I should've volunteered to work. At least I wouldn't be alone. My friends in both Cottonwood and Marin all have plans. My film team canceled because Rob has some important meeting. The rest of the group went to the IMAX theater in the city, and I wasn't exactly invited. We aren't that good of friends yet, though if I'd pushed it when Cass called me, I know they would've taken me along. Even Mac, Mom, and Austin are gone, driving to meet Dad halfway so Mac can see him this weekend. Mom and Austin won't be back till after midnight.

LONDON: You have plans now.

This actually worries me more than excites me. Though, okay, there's a bubble of hope brewing in my stomach. I want to do something fun, really fun, and how do you do that alone?

> ME: But I can't really do anything. My mom and stepdad
> are gone.
> LONDON: Call and ask to stay the night at my house.

Mom has met London a few times now. London finds our house and family "quaint" and "like a family on TV," which is just weird to me.

> ME: Um, okay. I'll try. But we aren't really staying at your
> house?
> LONDON: Eventually. Don't ask anything else, it's a
> surprise. And that way you won't have to lie.

"Where are you?" I ask when Mom answers the phone.

"We just met your dad and are heading back. But we were thinking of seeing a movie in Vacaville. Are you okay? Would you mind being alone till pretty late?"

"No, I don't mind." I pause a moment, crossing my fingers. "But London called and wants me to stay the night." *That isn't lying*, I tell myself.

"Um, are her parents home?"

The phone cuts out just then.

"I don't know, but I'd guess so."

"What? I couldn't hear you."

The call suddenly is lost, and I wonder if this is God looking out for my social life, or somebody else.

Mom calls back and says, "Just be careful, do the right things, can you hear me?"

"Yes."

"I'm in a bad spot . . . call you . . . leave a number to . . . love you, sweetie."

Wow, she must feel pretty bad for leaving me alone tonight.

"I love you too!"

ME: She said yes.
LONDON: Excellent! Now dress up a bit and be ready
    around ten. We'll pick you up.
ME: What does dress up mean? And WE? Who's we? What
    are we doing?
LONDON: Don't ask, just look good.

I fling open my newly organized clothes and start pulling things out.

Music plays loudly—a mixed CD of funky music that Frankie made for me. One song is about loving shoes, then Queen sings about riding a bicycle. Who wouldn't dance around the room with dresses and coats as partners with those songs playing?

I try on clothes while occasionally typing to several friends from Cottonwood. Kate is leaving for a date with her secret boyfriend. She told her parents she was going to the movies with Meegan and Felicity.

My worries for Kate don't dampen this happy hyper emotion welling up inside me. Sort of like butterflies, or maybe the opposite of them, but the adrenaline rush makes me want to skydive or take the first flight to anywhere or dance all night at a salsa bar in some cool Latin city like Havana.

From life feeling terrible to it being the greatest thing in the universe—it's funny how quickly it changes. I want to breathe in life and let it pulse out every pore.

I match a black cotton dress that hangs loosely and covers the few pounds I've gained lately with some funky silver shoes and rhinestone earrings, but then I switch the rhinestones for fear that the rich girls will be wearing diamonds. Instead I wear a necklace made of a curled shell that I bought in Maui and some bangle bracelets. I click and send a pic to London for approval.

She sends back a picture of three thumbs up, and I wonder whose thumbs those might be. I only hope Mom doesn't call me anytime soon.

"I want this to be a night to remember," I say aloud to my favorite teddy bear, Blue, who has journeyed from childhood to near adulthood with me. He looks at me with all the loyalty of a dog.

LONDON: We're here!

A car honks from the driveway, and I grab a small clutch purse with gloss and twenty bucks.

As I rush out the front door and toward the black Lexus SUV, my legs shake with nervous energy. London hops out the passenger door, looking fabulous as always. Her red hair and her long legs shimmer in the light, and I wonder how she can look so perfect from head to toe. She hugs me and then leads me to the open passenger window.

"I'm sure you already know Brett." She points to the guy in the backseat.

I've met Brett a few times but don't know him well.

"But I don't think you've met Anthony Restiva."

"Hi," I say, suddenly worried about the two-couple scenario.

"Can you believe it?" she whispers, grabbing my arm. "Anthony."

Then it hits me that this is the guy, the one she stalks at school, much to my amazement. "How did you arrange this? And can I know what we're doing?"

London opens the back door, and we slide in while Brett switches to the passenger seat in front.

"The plans keep changing, actually. We were going to a club in the city." London laughs. "The look on your face! Don't worry, you don't need a fake ID or anything. My cousin owns three of the best clubs in Frisco. He lets me and my friends in whenever I want."

"But we aren't going there?"

"Maybe. First we're stopping by a party, maybe picking up Isa and Krista, then we'll decide. Brett wanted a beach party, but I look too good for beach and bonfires."

She laughs with all the joy and youth that pulses through me, and I settle back against the leather seat beside her. It's like we're movie stars or something.

We drive the winding roads with the subwoofers pounding through our backs, laughing and singing, until Anthony slows the car and parks along a driveway where a bunch of other cars are lined up.

"So who wants to be sober driver?" he asks, flipping the keys in his hand.

"Not Ruby," London says with a laugh.

"I won't have my license for three months," I say, then feel stupid.

"Since she can't be the driver, she won't be sober." Brett raises his eyebrows and smiles.

"Oh, I will be sober," I say with a slight nervous stutter.

"We'll see about that," Brett says.

"Don't worry, I'll take care of you," London assures me.

She threads her arm through mine and leads me up the brick driveway with perfect hedges and solar lights along the edge. The four of us walk forward like invincible beautiful things. This is how it feels anyway—that if I could see us from the outside, I would stop to watch the approach of four confident people ready to stretch our suits of youthfulness and breathe in the air of unlimited possibilities.

Who do I want to be? Who am I? These questions whisper in my ear with my every step toward the grand white house that looms before us. The music hits us halfway up the driveway. The clean brass outdoor lights shimmer with the vibrations.

Brett opens the front door without knocking, and when we walk in, there's no one around. If not for the deafening music and cars outside, I'd think we've come to the wrong place. The marble tiles clink beneath London's heels as we walk through an entry and hallway with chandeliers, framed art with individual lights shining on each, and several encased guitars. This house could be featured on one of those MTV shows where musicians and actors give tours of their homes.

We follow Brett, who walks without hesitation past a grand staircase and a living room that looks like a gallery of white with plush carpet, furniture, and authentic-looking tribal statues. Three huge photographs depict three women in various fashion poses. Their bronze skin is flawless, and I wish to study the prints longer, but the others are moving toward the kitchen.

London covers her ears beneath a stereo speaker set flush with the wall. The kitchen too is empty of people, but through a wall of glass we see "the party."

"Nice," London says as the music fades between songs. "I've always heard Ally puts on a great party."

The music rises fast, and as I watch, two girls in bikinis dance on a table and a group of people push a fully clothed guy into the pool. I suddenly want to bolt back along the marble tiles to the car.

"Hey, Ruby, want a beer?" Brett yells with his face in the refrigerator.

I nearly yell back, "I'm not drinking," and then imagine the music stopping and me shouting this. Wouldn't that be my luck? Instead I shake my head when he holds two cans up.

Anthony motions for us to follow, and we step outside. Once the glass doors are closed behind us, the music isn't as overpowering, though it's still loud.

"There's Ally—we'll go say hi in a minute," London says, motioning toward a girl sitting on the edge of the pool.

Her wet dark skin and long black hair glisten in the light. She's one of the models in the photographs inside the house, I realize.

I walk close to London. "I didn't bring my swimsuit," I whisper.

She says, "They didn't either," and motions to several girls in their lace bras sitting in the bubbling hot tub. A waterfall cascades down to another hot tub full of people.

And as we step down to the lower pool level, I know without a doubt I'm way out of my league.

I'm sitting in the pool house bathroom when someone knocks on the door. "Just a minute," I say and turn on the brass faucet.

So far I've been asked to play "quarters," try the "beer bong," and play a game of "shot poker." So these are drinking games. The drugs are being used inside the house. This is obvious by those returning, wiping their noses or exhibiting sudden personality shifts.

Cocaine and ecstasy are the drugs of choice, London tells me. "Don't worry, Ruby. I went through rehab and intense counseling from age twelve to fourteen."

Is this supposed to be reassuring?

There's not much to do when you say no to all of that, except sit in the hot tub in your underwear, which I'd never do—especially since I wore my favorite but faded black bra and my blue penguin underwear that says CUTIE PIE. Some of the girls prance around in expensive and very small lingerie that definitely gets the guys' attention.

For a while London and I sat beside Brett as he played shot poker, then she disappeared with Anthony just when I wanted to ask if we could leave soon. When I went to the pool house bathroom, I decided to just stay there awhile.

Another knock hits the door. Guess my time is up.

"It's about time," a girl shouts, laughing hysterically when I open the bathroom door. Three girls are waiting, drunk and laughing.

I act as if I'm still the confident, self-assured girl I was when approaching the house with London, Anthony, and Brett. But where do I go now? I'm having flashbacks of my first lunch hour at Marin High. And yet this is painfully harder. When I look through the glass window to the shot poker game, I see that Brett is gone.

"Hey, come on in!" a guy shouts from the hot tub, motioning me over. The music is no longer enjoyable but is hurting my head.

"No thanks," I say.

And then I see Blair.

We spot each other at the same time, so there's no way to avoid her. Her look of surprise quickly turns to a smirk. I don't have to imagine what she's thinking.

She walks directly over to me. "So the little Christian is out partying?"

"Just because I'm at a party doesn't mean I'm not a Christian. And I'm not 'partying.'"

She brushes back a strand of long blonde hair, and I wonder how she does her makeup so model-perfect. I've never seen any-one with such sophistication at age sixteen.

London comes close. But Blair has perfected it. I feel like a cutesy schoolgirl compared to her.

"How can you be a good witness here, Ruby?" Her smooth voice conveys a note of exaggerated concern. "Or are you out proselytizing? Praying for the sinners, trying to save their mortal souls?"

"You think you know a lot about Christianity."

"I do know about it. I went to Sunday school and church when I was young."

"And what happened?"

She laughs. "I found the truth."

"What truth was that?"

She comes close to me, and I catch a whiff of alcohol on her breath. "The truth that God is not who you think He is."

"Then who is He?" And it strikes me that we're having a theological debate in the middle of a high school party.

"Let's just say He isn't who my Sunday school teacher said He was . . . not when my brother became an addict, or my father who was a deacon in the church became a very wealthy business-man and now has a wife who isn't much older than me."

I falter then, seeing a glint of pain in her eyes. What do I say to that?

Thankfully, before I'm forced into a response, a guy inter-rupts us. I think my mouth drops a little when I look at him. He could seriously be a runway model, has that European thing going on with a chiseled jaw and a chest cut like an Italian statue. I didn't know guys like that existed in normal life. And I'd guess he's at least twenty-five.

"Hey, baby, you promised," he says to Blair.

What is this, a party for the beautiful people?

She smiles and kisses him lightly. "I did promise, didn't I? Excuse us."

She takes a few steps away and slides her dress over her head, revealing a white and silver bikini underneath. Blair is the female equivalent to the guy with her, and she moves in a way that shows she knows it. Everyone stares as she and the guy walk to the upper hot tub.

And I'm again left standing alone. A yearning for home comes over me, and I wonder how far it would be to walk.

"Ruby!" a voice calls through the music that has thankfully changed from rap to eighties. I glance around until I see Brett beyond the swimming pool near a gazebo.

"Ruby!" he calls louder.

I weave around several couples making out on lounge chairs, several guys lined up to do cannonballs into the pool, and a girl who dances alone on a table like she's in some hallucinogenic state.

Brett falls over a small hedge before I reach him. His head is beneath a bush, which makes him appear headless for a moment.

I sit him up but can't get him up any farther.

"I'll never drink again," he says.

"That's good, Brett."

"You're so smart not to drink. Or are you a goody-goody?"

"Why don't we get you back to the house, or at least onto a chair?"

But he doesn't move, and I have to keep him from falling back over. And then he starts to vomit. The stench makes my stomach convulse, and I want to leave him, but he begs me not to.

"Ruby, you're so pretty. Like a ruby." Then he laughs, and I nearly throw up from his breath.

I could call Mom, but oh, I can envision that scenario. She's always said I should call if I'm in such a situation, to never ride with someone who's been drinking, to never ever drink and drive . . . *You can call me, Ruby; you won't get into trouble.*

Yeah, right, I think. She'd never let me out of the house again. A weariness sweeps over me at the idea of seeing her. Austin would surely come as well. They'd have those disappointed expressions.

My brother is in Cottonwood—no help there.

And I know Aunt Jenna's working early at the Underground again, and she lives too far away.

I try remembering how long it took us to get here from my house, but visions of being kidnapped, getting lost, and wandering for miles in the cold keep me from that plan.

A guy appears on the gazebo roof yelling, "King of the Mountain!" A group runs over and coaxes him down.

Brett starts vomiting again, and it's reconfirmed that I'd make a terrible nurse. I prop him up and walk a few steps away to give him privacy . . . at least that's what I tell myself.

"Ruby!" he calls again. He's getting sicker, and it's kind of freaking me out. London and Anthony are nowhere to be seen.

At least a half hour passes before Brett is finally able to get up. I halfway carry him to a lounge chair. Blair walks up in her bikini with a drink in her hand.

"Need some help?"

"No, I think he'll be okay. Have you seen London?"

"I think she's busy right now," Blair says with a slight smile.

"Okay," I say, wondering what I do until she's not busy.

"This is for you," Blair says, holding the drink out to me.

"No thanks."

"I didn't ask."

"I'm the designated driver," I lie, adding to the others I've been telling lately.

"Drink it."

"Why?"

"You're at a party, so have a drink."

The male model from the hot tub comes over. "Who's this?"

"This is Ruby," Blair says dramatically. "Ruby, this is Jason."

"I didn't know Blair had any girlfriends."

Blair gives him a smirk. "Ruby and I were about to have a drink together. Why don't you get yourself one, and one for me? This is hers."

"Sure."

"I'm not drinking with you," I say as the guy leaves. "What's the big deal if I drink or don't?"

"That's what I was wondering," Blair says.

The guy comes right back with two glasses, and he and Blair sit down. She motions for me to sit as well.

I remain standing, but the drink is set on the table in front of me.

"You should tell Jason about yourself, Ruby."

I glance around. No help in sight. Brett is passed out on the chair. London is still missing in action.

"Let's have a toast to Ruby," Blair says and raises her glass.

"To Ruby," Jason says, reaching to clink my glass with his. "Come on, girl." His voice is silky smooth.

And so I pick up the glass and drink it. It stings down my throat and feels hot in my stomach.

Blair has a strange expression on her face—something of evil triumph, but with something else behind it. "Let's get another round."

And I feel the defeat all through me. If I'd chosen to have a drink myself, that would be one thing. But to be forced into it, to cave in to Blair and see the look of satisfaction on her face is more than I can take.

"I'm leaving. Thanks for the drink," I say as casually as possible.

But inside the house, I can't find my purse and jacket. Someone tells me that they were all moved into a bedroom, and so I go searching down the hall.

"Can I get you another drink?" someone says, coming up behind me.

It's Jason, still in his wet shorts with no shirt. I can't even look at him, he makes me so nervous.

"No, I'm fine." I look around him to see if Blair is following. "I'm just looking for my purse and then I'm leaving."

"I'll help you. Probably in one of the bedrooms." He walks by me, giving me a coy look as he passes close. He opens the first door just a crack and motions me over. "Look at this."

"What?" I ask and look inside. It's dark, so I can't see anything at first. Jason comes up behind me, his body only inches from mine, and then I see the couple on the bed. I push back quickly and away from him, which makes him laugh.

"That was quite a sight," he says with a wide grin. "Maybe we'd better knock next time. Or maybe not."

He comes closer, walking with even and steady steps, staring into my eyes. "You intrigue me, Ruby."

"Why?" I say, taking a few steps back.

"I don't know. There's something about you. Your wide-eyed innocence, or is it naiveté? I'm not sure, but it's so attractive. You aren't jaded or fake."

He's close now, and I feel like one of those mice caught by the mesmerizing gaze of a cobra. My feet won't move, my voice won't work. Finally I say, "Where's Blair?"

"She sent me to check on you. She hates you, you know."

"That's pretty clear."

"She hates everyone. Even me." Jason laughs at that.

My heels touch the wall. I didn't realize I'd been slowly backing up.

"I can give you a ride home."

"It's okay. I'd better find my purse." I turn to move past him, but he takes hold of my arms.

"You're such an adorable girl," he says, and then kisses me.

I pull away with the taste of his soft lips and a hint of sweet alcohol on my lips. *God, help me.*

And then I'm out the front door with Jason calling behind me. I run down the driveway, and when I reach the street, I start walking and walking. My feet ache not long after I get beyond the line of cars. The road slants downward, and my heels are slippery on the damp road, but still I walk. It's not for a long time that I realize my purse, cell phone, and jacket are still at the house. There's no going back now.

The residential neighborhood drops down into a commercial area of shops and restaurants, but they're all closed. Then, like going around a corner, the night turns colder. The sky shows nothing but darkness. The fog must be blotting out the stars.

A few cars pass, one slowing and making my heart beat so fast that I can hardly hear anything. I want to take off my shoes and run, but the car accelerates and drives away. If only I would hear London's voice calling from the car, and I wouldn't be alone. I can't believe she left me there on my own.

Finally I see a phone booth by the dull glow of a far-off streetlight. It makes me walk faster despite the pain in my feet. But when I get there, there's only a dangling wire. Fear and loneliness sweep over me. Should I try finding my way back? Should I hide somewhere till morning?

Shivers course through me as I walk again. I can't get the shivering to stop. Then I see an all-night gas station, lights blazing ahead of me like the beacon of a lighthouse for a lost ship.

This pay phone works, but it takes a few minutes to figure out how to call collect. Then I pray Mom answers the phone.

She has her fake awake voice. "Ruby?"

I know she hates late-night calls.

"Ruby, where are you? Why are you calling collect?"

"I'm at a pay phone."

"A pay phone where?" The faux calm has left her voice.

"I don't know for sure. There's a gas station here. I'm outside of it."

I hear Austin's mumbled questions in the background.

"You're supposed to be staying the night at London's. Are you near her house? Where is she?"

"She's not here." I don't even want to explain this.

A creepy guy walks into the gas station, staring at me all the way in.

"Mom, just come get me."

"We need to figure out where you are. Is there a phone number there?"

"Why?"

"Austin says we can call from the cell phone and keep you on the line while we drive to find you."

"There's no number. I can ask inside the gas station."

"No, just wait. Do you see a street sign?"

"Yeah. First and Corte Madera. And the gas station is called the Pit Stop."

"Okay, just stay right there. Maybe you should go inside. Austin will use his GPS to find you and we'll be right there."

"Okay."

It's probably only fifteen minutes, but it feels like an hour before I see their headlights approach. I get in the backseat almost before they stop the car.

"Can we talk about this tomorrow?" I say before Mom can dive into her interrogation.

"Are you okay?" she asks in a worried tone.

"Yeah." I slide off my shoes and feel immediate pain and relief.

"Have you been drinking?"

I want to explain but instead just say, "Yeah, sort of."

Silence. Which can actually be worse than an immediate response. An eruption may be brewing.

"Mom, can you ground me or yell at me in the morning? I just want to go home."

She starts to respond, but Austin puts a hand on her arm. She's silent a moment, then says, "Okay."

Closing my eyes, I want to sleep right here as the heater slowly touches the cold that has settled deep in my bones.

We get home and I go straight to my room after thanking

Mom and Austin for picking me up. A few minutes later I hear the bathwater running, and Mom peeks into my room.

"That's for you if you want it."

I realize that I'm still shivering. "Yeah, thanks, Mom."

"We'll need to talk about this."

"I know."

"But for tonight, I'm just glad you're safe and at home."

I nod. I don't even know what to say.

chapter eighteen

I stay in bed till late morning. Mom brings her three-page letter into my room along with breakfast and my jacket and purse, which London dropped by. I was hiding under the covers when she arrived, not ready to face the day, not ready to tell one of my new friends how angry I am at her.

Mom must have spent hours typing up her letter that lists and explains my punishment. I act like it's harsh with my dejected look, but it's way less than I expected.

The letter says that because I called and left the party, because I was honest about drinking, and because it was a terrible experience for me, my punishment isn't very severe.

But because I lied, or sort of lied by implication—which is still a lie, Mom says—I must have some consequences.

For one week:

—No cell phone

—No Internet except for school use

—No friends over

—Limited telephone

—Can go to film group

—Can go to church youth group outings

—Must go to school and attend family events

"Wait a minute." As I awaken more, it suddenly sinks in. "A whole week without my cell phone or going online? How will I call you from school and work?"

"I know when to pick you up after school. And the coffee-house has a phone."

At that moment my phone beeps.

"Go ahead and check your messages, then tell your friends you won't be available."

"But . . ." And I think of my friends in Cottonwood, and oh, oh, what if Kaden finally e-mails?

She must see the panic on my face. "You can check your messages once a day to see if there's some kind of an emergency. But that's it."

"But . . ." And I fall back onto my pillow with my plate still balanced in my hands. "Okay."

Mom leaves, and the quiet of the room surrounds me.

I skim through the messages on my phone. Kate telling about her date, friends in Cottonwood saying hi. I don't really read them. Then London asking where I am, if I'm okay, followed by a long list of apologies and the promise to make up for her desertion by treating me to a full day at the spa (and I know I'll end up forgiving her in a few days). There's even a text from Brett: Help me!

I don't read further, just toss the phone onto the blanket beside me. It's not a bad quiet in my room; it's sort of peaceful. After I eat the breakfast Mom brought up, I take another long bath and decide to work on my room. I hang up all the clothes I pulled out when looking for something to wear last night. In the afternoon it warms up outside. I open the balcony doors, then retrieve my easel from the garage and set it up on the balcony. This week would be a good time to paint, since I can't do much else anyway.

The picture of Beatrice—maybe Aunt Betty—in the corner of my mirror catches my attention often throughout the day. And I wonder about the stories of my aunt's life that are long before my years.

I hear Mom coming up the stairs. "No, she isn't moving in with you because of this. I just thought you should know so you can talk to her. She's making friends and doing well."

There's a knock on my door, and Mom hands me the phone. "It's your dad," she says. "I need to talk to him again when you're done."

"Hi, Dad."

"So I hear you had a scary experience."

"Yeah."

"Your mom said you went to a little party last night. And you tried walking home?"

"Yes."

"You need to come up and stay with me for a while," he says, and I can't help but smile.

Dad is so predictable. There's no doubt that he was talking big before hearing my voice, telling Carson and Tiffany how he'd ground me for the next year or something to that effect. Now he's good old loving Dad.

"Maybe I'll come up next weekend," I say. And suddenly I miss him terribly. I want to see him now. Part of me is a little hurt that he isn't angry with me for all of this, or for moving away. Doesn't he need me the way he needs Carson?

"Carson wants to talk to you."

"Great," I say with a sigh.

"What were you thinking?" my brother says in his grouchy, parental Carson voice. He's often harder on me than Dad is.

"What do you care?" I shoot back, which actually makes him stop talking.

"Okay, that was cold." I sigh again. "I had a terrible night, I'm grounded, and I don't need a lecture from you. As if you don't go to parties once in a while. You just never had anything like this happen."

"You have a point."

I hear a slight chuckle, but then the second line beeps and I miss what he says. "Hang on, someone is calling."

"Is this Ruby?"

Oh great, it's Grandma Hazel. I want to tell her I'll call her back but decide to get this over at once.

When I tell Carson who's on the other line, he laughs again and gives a long whistle. "Okay, I'll leave you alone. You'll be punished enough after that phone call."

Grandma Hazel and I get through the preliminary small talk, and then she jumps in deep.

"I hear that you've made friends with a homosexual. And also that you were drinking?"

I'm going to kill Mom for telling Dad about the party, and Carson for telling Dad about Frankie, and Dad for telling his mother about them both. Why does everything have to spread all over this family?

"Yes, Grandma."

"So those things are true?"

She sounds truly horrified, and I worry about her age and adding Grandma-killer to my list of wrongs. But what else can I say but the truth?

"Grandma, my friend is a very nice person, even though, yes, he is a homosexual." I want to laugh at the way we're pronouncing *homo-sex-u-al.*

"Oh, sweetie. I remember when you were so close to the Lord. I remember seeing you praise God as just a little girl. Don't lose your faith down in that big, vile city of San Francisco."

"I'm not losing my faith, Grandma. And you know, there's something vile everywhere in the world."

"Oh, but you can't surround yourself with the world and not think you'll not be affected. And the whole hippie, druggie, homosexual thing began down in that city. I've been so worried about all of you down there."

"Okay, Grandma."

There's no sense in trying to convince her. My first day of being grounded started off not so badly, but now as I sit through a half hour of lecturing, I'm ready to kill someone.

On Sunday I'm stir-crazy and happy to go to church. But what I keep wondering is if Jason will tell Blair that he kissed me—if a kiss is what you call it. His lips connected to mine, though technically, I didn't want them to.

In the church we're trying out today—this one more

traditional and boring—I'm reminded of my recent questions about God and what I believe. Grandma Hazel thinks I'm losing my faith. Blair thinks I'm like Billy Graham in female form. And I don't know what I am.

At school the next day, I successfully avoid Blair even through the lunch hour. Frankie finds me hiding in the library reading a book about filmmaking and bursts out laughing when he sees me. He thinks the whole party and my restrictions are something that should be depicted in a Norman Rockwell painting, if Norman were still alive to paint the all-American Ruby of the twenty-first century.

"It's so deliciously you!" he says, throwing his hands in the air and laughing so loudly that the librarian threatens him with a bright red face of anger. "Oh, and by the way, you'd better keep avoiding Blair."

"I'm not avoiding her. I had to go by the office to change my International Cooking class to Film so I can get out early for some of our shoots, and then I remembered a book I wanted to find . . . Wait, how did you know I'm avoiding Blair?"

"'Cause I know you kissed Jason."

"I didn't kiss him! He kissed me."

"I know that too, but I wanted to see your reaction."

"He only did it to get a reaction out of Blair—at last that's what I think."

Frankie sits on the edge of the table. "Yeah, girlfriend, that guy may be incredibly hot, but he doesn't have a lot of assets upstairs, if you know what I mean." He suddenly jumps up. "Oh, there's Blair."

I startle and fling the filmmaking book off the table as I look around. The room is empty. Frankie laughs.

"Evil—you are seriously evil, Frankie Klarken."

He gives a long Count Dracula *mwahwahwah* laugh.

The librarian storms over and picks up the book from the floor, glaring at me as if I dropped her baby. "Both of you, out of here. Now!"

The house phone rings late in the night, and I grab the one by my bed. Caller ID shows Kate's cell number.

"Hey, were you sleeping?" she asks as I settle back into the warmth of my bed.

After school I fell asleep, so now I've been awake, reading about film and writing in my journal while listening to music. It's strangely nice and lonely being grounded from communication.

"Sort of, but not really." I listen for a moment in case the ring woke Mom up. "But I'm not supposed to talk 'cause of . . . you know why."

"Yeah, I know."

The sound of her voice makes me think she's been crying.

"But I really need to talk to you."

"What's wrong?"

"I'm just going to say it so we don't draw this out."

"Okay."

"James and I had sex."

I sit straight up in my bed. "You're kidding, right?" *Please let this be a terrible joke.*

She doesn't respond for a long moment.

"Why?" I say loudly, falling back hard against the headboard.

"*Why? That's* not what I expected. More like *What? How? When?* But not *Why?*"

"I thought you were waiting for the right person. Until you were older, until you were in love."

"I did." There's a defensive tone in her voice now.

"You did want to wait, or James is the right person?"

"I don't know."

My mind can't even make sense of this. I stare out toward the balcony where soft light comes through in gentle streams. This can't be true.

"Ruby?"

And the fearful tone in her voice sends away all the questions and angry feelings. This is Kate's life-changing moment, one of those momentous passages like graduation, when we got our periods, marriage, first love, first sex . . . My best friend has had sex.

She's only fifteen years old, and then I realize how that sounds like an old judgmental woman. I don't want to be judgmental. And it's not like we don't know a lot of people even younger than fifteen having sex. It didn't bother me when it was them.

Kate has had sex!

"I'm not ready for this," I whisper without meaning to. A sadness washes over me.

"I know you aren't."

"Sorry, I didn't mean to make this about me."

"Don't worry about it. It's not really a big deal."

"And yet it's one of the biggest deals of your life."

"People make too much of it."

And for that, I feel even sadder. Kate's not going to tell me her true feelings right now anyway. It's like the time she stole a pack of gum because some kids dared her to do it. When she told me, I was worried the police would arrive at any second, while she acted like she hadn't done anything wrong. Hours later she started crying when I won hopscotch three times in a row and started walking down the road. I asked where she was going and she yelled, "I'm taking the gum back."

We went together. I wanted to sneak the gum onto the rack, but Kate walked straight up to the cashier and plopped the pack onto the counter. She still had tears in her eyes.

The clerk nodded and said, "Thank you."

Kate nodded back and walked out of the store with me standing there gaping.

Kate.

But this wasn't a pack of gum . . . and she couldn't take it back.

"How did it happen? Are you okay?" I try sounding interested, not angry. Why am I angry?

"Yeah, I'm okay. You know I've been seeing him for a while now."

Why didn't I talk to her more about him when she was here? Why didn't I see this coming? Why didn't she tell me, ask me if she should do this? What kind of best friend am I?

"You've been dating less than a month!"

"He's going to Shasta College and transferring to a state university next year. He and a longtime friend have an apartment—just like we want to do in a few years. Meegan's sort of dating his roommate, so we've been over there a lot."

"Meegan," I say, rubbing my forehead and walking to the balcony doors.

Meegan and I don't like each other. That Kate is hanging out with her disturbs me. Meegan started smoking pot with her older sister in seventh grade. Now she's graduated to sophisticated drugs. But Kate and Meegan's families have been close since they were toddlers.

"James's uncle brought Jet Skis, and I rode with him all day. He was totally into me, showing me how to drive. We explored all over Shasta Lake, just the two of us. He . . ."

I feel tired suddenly, and I don't want to hear more of this story.

"What did Meegan say?"

"She said welcome to being an adult."

"She would say that." Then I pause. "I'm sorry. Do you feel like an adult?"

"No way. I feel exactly the same."

But I can't imagine such a thing not affecting her, or anyone really. But then, what experience do I have? Kissing is as far as I've traveled down that road.

"What are you going to do now?"

"Do? I'm not going to *do* anything. I'm in love with James."

Kate won't analyze all of this like I will. She'll probably wonder at her emotions, be surprised by them, and then we'll talk more about it. For now, she has told me. That's what she needed to do, and now she's done it. Suddenly my love for her floods over me, and I wish I could give her a long hug.

"Listen. Let's talk more tomorrow then. I'll ask special permission from Mom."

"Sounds good."

"Just . . ." I want to say, *Don't have sex again. Be careful! Are you using protection? Don't be dumb. Why don't you dump that jerk? Stay away from Meegan.* But of course I don't. "Just know that I love you."

I can hear her smile.

"Thanks. That's what I needed to hear. I love you too."

There's no way I can sleep after that conversation. I can't fully process all the sudden changes in our lives.

The open balcony doors send in a stream of cold air and moonlight. I pull a sweatshirt over my head and step onto the cold tile. The railing already has a slight dampness of morning dew, though it's many more hours before dawn.

The garden is filled with light and darkness, and I wish as I so often do for the skill to paint such a scene in the way I want. My paintings are nothing close to what I want them to be. Kate would laugh at that, probably bring up my pottery wheel disaster.

But with film, it's as if the puzzle pieces come together. So here I am discovering new things about myself, finding direction, even while making mistakes and being completely confused about other things. My relationship with my family is all different. I'm not sure where God fits in my life. I have friendships that maybe God wouldn't want, and yet I really love Frankie especially and even London.

Some things are completely messed up. Other things are finally found.

Maybe it's the ceramic gnome in the garden sitting beneath a moonlight glow, but I suddenly think of Mac's imaginary friend, Beano. Beano went on vacations with us to Yellowstone

National Park, camping along the Oregon coast, and many other places. At night he listened to whatever book Mom was reading to Mac. Beano was around years longer than Carson and I thought he should have been. My mom always thought it was cute and imaginative, telling us to stop teasing Mac about it.

How strange that I think of Beano now. I wonder where he is. I wonder if he's here.

I'll have to ask Mac.

Sometimes I wish I could go back and be a little kid again. I'd take Kate with me, and my brothers. Beano can come too. We'll be happily insulated in our childhood, safe from growing up and from the mistakes we make that affect the rest of our lives.

I'll be in Cottonwood this weekend. It's the place of my childhood. But with the years of change and over a month living in Marin, I wonder how to return to my home that isn't really home anymore.

chapter nineteen

So this is what it's like to be in a time machine.

It's been one month since I left Cottonwood, but it seems like years. When the familiar signs come into view—MAIN STREET, BOWMAN ROAD EXIT—it's like I've gone back in time and only I know it. The rest of the world has no idea how much everything has changed, what's been occurring in the time warp. To all of them it's been the blink of an eye.

Well, it's something like that.

Mom stops by the ballpark, which some people call "the largest church in town" due to the dedication and sports worship that goes on in the bleachers and out on the fields.

The dirt parking lot is packed, the three fields all in progress, from tiny players in oversized uniforms to players who hit and throw like pros, though they're all under twelve. My third cousin Jimmy is playing, so the ballpark is the switching place for me to leave Mom and go to Dad.

"Why do we have to meet here?" I ask again. "I hardly even know Jimmy."

I can't even remember the last time I talked to him, but since he's my dad's cousin's son and Dad likes to watch a ballgame under any excuse, this is the plan, as Mom reminds me again.

I can't believe it's been over a month since I saw Dad. Terrible as this sounds, it's almost like I nearly forgot him in a way.

"There's your dad's truck," Mom says, and Austin parks behind it.

Mom and Austin are going with Carson up to Oregon to visit friends after they drop Mac and me off.

We unload our stuff into the back of Dad's shiny red truck, say good-bye to Mom and Austin, then go searching for Dad. I spot him standing by the bleachers, his gaze going over the parking lot and then landing on me.

Dad takes me in his arms and raises me off the ground. I'm little next to him, and suddenly I want to cry like a child—even worse than when I saw Kate when she came to Marin.

"There's my girl. It's about time you came to see me." His voice is like home, and he gives me another squeeze.

Mac hugs Dad too, then sees one of his friends and rushes off to play.

Dad hands me a bag of sunflower seeds. His hands are thick and calloused. He winks and puts his arm around my shoulder, pulling me close.

"Where's Tiffany?" I ask, not seeing her in the bleachers.

"She's working most of the weekend, so I'm all yours," he says with a smile that wrinkles lines near his eyes.

A deep love for him fills me, and an entire month of missing him rises. I follow him up into the bleachers, saying hello to several parents I recognize. Dad has two bleacher cushions waiting for us, and we sit and spit shells into an empty soda can. My mouth is soon salty and raw, reminding me of the years when Carson played and we'd sit like this, eating seeds.

"How's city life?" he asks, then stands up suddenly. "Oh, did you see that hit?"

"It's good," I say when he sits back down. I'm not even interested in the game, but the nearness of Dad is surprisingly comforting. "I'm getting more involved with that film group I told you about."

"So you're gonna make movies?"

"Yeah, that's what we're doing. Maybe you can come down and see some?"

"Can't you bring them up here?"

"Um, I don't know. They put on this big Premiere Night at the Underground—you know, the coffeehouse and cinema that Aunt Jenna owns. It'll be next month."

"We might be able to come down for that."

And with the *we* I think how awkward it'd be to have my dad and Tiffany with my mom and Austin all at the same event. We've never had anything with all of them together except for pickup/drop-off things.

Grandma Hazel arrives, and we wave her up. I spot Grandpa Joel talking with his usual animation with another old-timer. My grandparents on my father's side look like a poster version of those cute old couples. But though Grandma Hazel looks cute, she's usually as sour as the green apples she grows in her front orchards that she always wants me to eat.

Dad gives up his cushion, and she sits in front of me, patting my knee in greeting. My nose fills with the scent of talcum powder.

"Oh, I think you've grown, and you don't have on as much eyeliner as you did the last time I saw you. That is a big improvement."

"Thanks, Grandma."

Dad winks at me.

"Did you listen to your grandma about what I talked to you about?"

"Yes, Grandma."

"There aren't any gangs down there, are there?"

"No, quite the opposite."

"What's the opposite?" Dad asks, prying himself away from the game.

"The school I go to is mostly filled with very well-off kids."

Grandma gives her typical stern expression. "Don't let them intimidate you. You stand up to them and let your light shine. The rich have a harder time coming to Jesus, you know."

"Yeah, the whole eye of the needle thing," I mumble and suddenly wish Carson were here. Carson enjoys getting Grandma riled up by telling her about the evils of the world that he's supposedly heard about, or mixing up Scripture to get her flustered.

Dad pours more seeds into my hands. "Are you still getting good grades?"

"Yeah."

"No boyfriends, right?"

"Not yet," I say with a smile.

"You don't need no city boy," he teases. "Let's find you a rancher with thousands of acres, and then your brother and I will move there with you. You can have ten little kids and grow your own garden."

"Okay, Dad. I'd be really happy doing that."

The thing is, I don't think Dad is really joking when he says things like that. I wonder if I disappoint him a little with my love of art, the city, culture, and travel. Those interests make me more like Mom than like him. And since they're divorced, does he dislike this part of me?

"Are you getting involved at a church yet? Does your mother attend church?" Grandma Hazel asks with the look of perpetual disapproval she wears when she asks about Mom.

"Yes, she and Austin attend church."

"What kind of church?"

"Hey, Mom," Dad says with a serious note beneath his light tone. "Let's watch the game or talk about other things."

"If you'd attend church more too, young man . . ." She stands. "I'll go get your grandpa to stop talking and come see his granddaughter. "

She leaves, and Dad puts his arm around me. "So what do you want to do this weekend? It's all for you and your brother."

"Whatever you want to do. It doesn't have to be anything special. But, Dad, I want to see my friends too. Can Kate stay over part of the time?"

The soft lines on his tanned face are deeper than I remember. Even with his hardware store, Dad often works beneath the sun, so he's perennially brown on his arms, face, and neck. We tease him about his white legs and chest when summer comes and he first reveals them. I move close to let someone by and catch a whiff of his aftershave, the Brut he's worn since I was little.

"Whatever you want, sweetie. You know I'll only ever have one little girl." He kisses the top of my head like I'm all of six years old.

"I know, so go ahead and spoil me rotten."

After the game, we go out for pizza and then rent DVDs. Mac and Dad fall asleep on the couch. When my stepmom, Tiffany, gets home after midnight in her nursing scrubs, we make tea and talk about life in Marin.

Dad wakes up then and kisses me good night.

"I miss you. I really do," he says as he heads to bed.

"I miss you too, Dad."

"Wake up, wake up!" Voices part the fog around my sleep. A group of faces stare down at me with a room in the background that I don't recognize. Then I see Kate smiling and laughing. I still don't know where I am, then I spot Tiffany's sewing machine in the corner and the dresser and computer that Dad gave me.

I'm at Dad's. And my friends are here—Felicity, Izzie, Jeffers, Claire, and then I see Nick leaning against the doorjamb. And seeing him, I suddenly feel that old attraction rise up. Oh, but he's in my room with a bunch of other people, and what the heck do I look like?

"What's going on?" I try sinking into the pillow and covers.

"We're taking you to breakfast, right now."

"You are not."

"We are!"

I peek out of the covers. "Okay, let me get dressed real fast then."

"Nope. You have to come just like that."

Ugh, I know there's no winning this one, despite all pleas and protests. I've been party to six different Rise & Go outings that first started with my church youth group in junior high. Usually near the unsuspecting friend's birthday, we'd talk to the parents ahead of time, then show up and drag the victim out of bed "as is" to a restaurant for breakfast.

Since my birthday is near the Fourth of July, my humiliation was always spared.

"Come on, my pajamas don't even match," I say, trying for any last-minute humanity.

"Did that stop you guys on my birthday when I was wearing those striped pajamas with the flap over the behind?" Kate asks.

"Let me at least use the bathroom."

"You have one minute."

As I'm brushing my teeth, someone bangs on the door. "Come on, in there."

"Brushing teeth!" I yell with a mouthful.

Pulling my hair into a ponytail, I cringe at my makeup-less face. *Be brave, be strong—if a guy doesn't like you for what you look like in the morning . . . yeah, right.*

My friends who drive can't drive other people for the first year of their license—California and its rules. My dad is always threatening to leave California because of the regulations on everything and go live in Idaho or Wyoming or the Yukon. So we pile into Dad's extended cab truck. I brush a strand of hair away from my face.

"Don't worry. You look good."

It's Nick, and he climbs over Kate to sit by me. She gives me the raised eyebrow and smile.

"So you like it down in Marin?"

"Yeah, it's pretty cool."

We make the usual small talk. He tells me about the baseball season starting and a football camp he's going to back east in the summer.

At the Old Town Eatery, Nick sits beside me there too. I'm the only one in pajamas, and a few people at their tables smile and know it's probably my birthday or something. Dad ends up eating with a guy he knows, leaving us "young folks" to spend time together.

My friends start catching me up on the month I've missed. There's a surprising amount of information. Breakups, rumors, things they've been doing, a cute new foreign exchange student from Germany. I don't know half the news, and it's fun hearing about it all. A lot has changed, and yet, strangely, nothing has changed. But being around the noise and energy of my friends, several I've known since kindergarten, is so unlike the way it feels with my new friends. It's like family, or being fully comfortable with your favorite people.

Our food arrives, and I dip into my favorite breakfast here—the eggs Benedict.

Nick leans close. "So guess what's happening next weekend."

"Next weekend?" The scent of his cologne draws me closer. Nick isn't the shy guy he was a month ago. He's flirty and comical as I've never seen him before.

"The prom," he says with a laugh.

"Ah, yes. Should be fun for you and Nikki," I say, all smiles, sugar, and spice.

"Why didn't I ask you out before? I think I was a late bloomer," he says, and his smile is pretty darn adorable.

I'm feeling all flirty now myself. "Yeah, pretty sad. The early bird catches the worm."

"What about second chances?"

"What kind of second chances?"

I glance at Kate, who is chatting with Felicity.

"Nikki has a boyfriend now. Everyone says she wants to go with him, but she feels bad dumping me after she wouldn't let me ask you."

"It's all so twisted."

"So what do you think?"

"What do I think? What are you asking, exactly?"

"Aren't letting me off easy, are you? Well, Ruby Madden, will you go to the prom with me?"

And before I even think it through, I say, "Why, yes, Nick Miller, I will go to the prom with you."

At last Kate and I have time together.

Dad takes Mac and Grandpa fishing in the afternoon, but I ask to go to Kate's instead. She wants me to meet James, but at the last minute he can't meet us at the mall, so we stay in her room and get into our pajamas, even though it's not even five o'clock.

I'm curious to meet James, since I've only seen pics that Kate sent me. He looks pretty cute, in a Kurt Cobain sort of way. But mainly, I wish the guy would disappear from her life. And I worry that my anger might rise on seeing him—I've actually thought of telling Carson and his friends. They'd take care of him even if they are younger.

Kate finally admits that he's almost twenty. She's fifteen.

"He makes me happy. With you gone, it's nice to have someone who really cares about me."

"Does he love you?" I ask. I'm torn between hating this guy before even meeting him and wanting to be open-minded. He can't be very smart; he could go to jail for this.

"He does, but we don't say that to each other."

"Then how do you know he does?"

She gives me the I-know-what-you're-doing-Ruby-so-stop-it look.

"I'm sorry. It's so weird for me. You have this older boyfriend suddenly, and you guys have had sex."

And from the look on her face, I see that it's happened more than once. I drop my head in my hands and groan.

"It's weird for me too. My life doesn't feel weird; it feels exactly perfect, except for all the lying I have to do to be with James. But your life. You have this whole new life, new friends— it's just as weird for me."

"But, Kate, I know you are making a huge mistake."

"And how would you know? I support everything you do, but you just assume I'm ruining my life when you don't even know what's been happening with me."

"I don't have to know much to know this isn't right for you. You're living a lie. And why would this guy want that too?"

"Oh, why would this guy want me? Is that what you mean?"

"That's not what I mean, and you know it. Does he want to stop hiding your relationship? Does he want to meet your parents and family? Have you met his friends and family?"

"I'm not talking to you about this."

But I can't stop. I want to save her from this, wish I'd already saved her. "Kate, I'm leaving till next weekend and the prom. We need to talk about this."

Kate stands and walks to the door. "Let's not talk till next weekend."

Home.

I'm not sure if I'm leaving it or going toward it as I ride in Dad's truck to meet Mom. Soon I'll leave Cottonwood and go to Marin like we left Marin on Friday and came to Cottonwood.

On the way to our meeting spot, we pass the cemetery, and I wonder if Little Tony is buried beneath the ground there. Country music is playing, which I can only tolerate when I'm with Dad. He sometimes breaks into singing with exaggerated movements. Mac always joins in, and that's when I turn my iPod up loudly. Usually. Once in a while, I sing along with Dad and Mac. But I don't tell anyone else that.

Mom isn't in the Holiday Market parking lot yet. We go inside the Elegant Bean for ice cream and coffee. The owner greets us and wants to hear about my new life in the city. When I was younger, I asked her for a job, and she always mentions that to me. After I tell her about working at the Underground, she says that if I move home, I'll have a job waiting.

Home—that illusive place.

Mom comes up behind us and gives Mac a hug.

"Did you have a good weekend?" she asks as she kisses me on the cheek. "No parties?"

I don't find it very funny to have any party reminders, which then makes us both smile.

"Hi," Mom says in a slightly awkward tone. That would mean Dad has returned from the restroom.

"Where's Austin?" my dad asks in his super-friendly voice.

Whenever Austin is around, Dad's overly friendly to the point I want to say, *It's okay that you don't want to be around him. He won't have his feelings hurt.*

"In the car," she says.

"I bet there's a lot of work to be done on Aunt Betty's place. Last time I was there, I was worried about that roof."

"She had it replaced a few years ago."

Mom doesn't ask about Tiffany. While Dad acts over-friendly, Mom just avoids the subject of Tiffany's existence when at all possible. Once she tried explaining it to me, that she didn't have hard feelings anymore and some other stuff, but I couldn't process it and didn't really want to. They are divorced, that's it, nothing more to say or explain or discuss.

Something always feels off-kilter when I see my parents together now. They are polite and cordial, like two professionals or strangers making a business transaction. We all have the memories of their love and years together. I remember, Mac remembers, and I know they have to remember sometimes too. But while we have the memories, we want to forget, or at least they surely do. We want to act like this is all okay, because strangely it is.

I'm not sure if it's weirder with the stepparents or without them. With the stepparents waiting outside in the cars and us in here, it's almost like we're a family again. Almost, but then, not really at all.

"I'd like to see the kids more," Dad says.

"I'd like to see Carson more too."

"We'll have to figure something out." Dad picks up Mac and turns him upside down, which makes him laugh hysterically. "We had a good weekend though, right, kids?"

"Yes!" Mac yells, and I smile at Dad.

Our coffees arrive on the counter, and Mom chats with the owner a few minutes.

Then Dad says, "Let's get your stuff from my truck."

Dad looks sad as he drives away, even with his smile and wave. The sadness was in his eyes, and tears form at the edges of my eyes. I want to yell at Austin to stop the car, and I'll grab my stuff and stay here. Instead I plug in my earbuds and turn my music up loud.

About a half hour later, with some distance behind us, we go through the usual answers to Mom's questions about our weekend. Mac always tells way too much, until I want to tape his mouth closed. Finally he winds down, especially because Mom isn't fully responsive. He puts in a movie on the handheld DVD player, and then it's silence and the road—and my music playing in my ears.

"Dad said you want to come back next weekend?" Mom asks in a tired tone.

"Yeah. Nick asked me to the prom."

"The prom? In one week? How are you supposed to get ready? I'm not sure if we are driving up again next weekend."

"All I need is a dress and shoes. One of the dresses Frankie gave me might just work." Though I really want that green dress. "Maybe we can meet Dad halfway."

"Maybe. What about film group? You missed this week, and aren't they filming next weekend?"

"Oh no," I say, hitting my forehead with the palm of my hand. "I forgot." How could I forget?

And for a while I don't want to go back to Aunt Betty's house, don't want the film group or anything else of Marin County. Then the closer I get toward Marin, the more Cottonwood disappears behind me. I wonder who came into the Underground over the weekend. I want to catch up on my MySpace messages. I wonder if Blair isn't going to confront me after all about Jason, though how could she hate me any worse than she already does?

Awhile later Mom closes her cell phone and motions for me to turn down my music. "Aunt Jenna called with a message for you."

"What?"

"It's about a certain guy," Mom says with a grin.

"Which certain guy?"

"One of your film guys."

"Which one? What did she say?"

"I guess he was asking about you."

"Asking what?"

"Where you were, what you've been doing."

"One of the guys from my film team?" I think of Rob, Sound Guy, Darren. "I'm not really interested in any of them."

"Oh, re-ally. Not interested in the yard-and-moving guy?"

"Kaden?"

"Yeah, that's the one." She smiles.

chapter twenty

"A unique opportunity has come up," Rob says at the special Monday night film group meeting he called unexpectedly. He presses his five fingers against the others and paces back and forth before us.

Once again Kaden is missing, so I doubt he's in this group—he hasn't been here since the first meeting I attended.

"We had a month and a half until the final premiere. However, I received a call from my father, and since then I've been working on something he proposed."

"What? Don't keep us in suspense, Rob," Olivia says with all the drama of a Broadway star.

"My father will be in Marin in two weeks. He asked if it was possible to have the premiere early, or a special movie release night with the other groups. He said there had to be at least four teams competing. He'd attend and bring several of his producer friends to watch the short movies and be the judges. And this is the exciting part: the group with the best film gets to spend a week on the set of the movie he's producing this summer; have a workshop with the director, crew, and actors; and . . ." Rob pauses for dramatic effect. "And receive $15,000 from a foundation he works with for the group's next project, with the possibility of additional backing to try getting the film into the indie festival circuit."

We stare first at Rob and then at each other with shocked expressions.

Cass jumps up and down, screaming.

"This is beyond cool," Darren Duke says, shaking his head.

I gaze around at the people in my group, some I'm getting to know and others I've barely talked with, and know that they deserve the excitement of this moment. They've been eating and breathing movies and moviemaking for years, some since they were young children. And here I am coming in on it so late and getting to be part of such an opportunity.

Something in me thinks that we'll win. I'm already imagining going on a movie set, maybe getting asked to be an extra—maybe I'll be one of those talents discovered by near accident. *Okay, calm down, Ruby,* I tell myself.

Rob continues with a satisfied grin on his face. "So I called the other three film groups in the area. They agreed to move up the date and join the competition. I only need our group to give the thumbs-up, though I obviously assumed it'd be a yes. But you have to know what we're facing. For the next two weeks, none of you will have a life. Everything outside of school and jobs needs to be eliminated. Since *Solitude* is the farthest in production, we're going to focus completely on that one and get it perfected. We've got to jump right on it. And this weekend we'll need someone's house for an all-weekend lock-in. I think we have a real shot at this."

"We need to get Kaden back," someone says.

"I'm working on that as well. He's had some family things going on in the past month, and he wasn't sure when he'd be with us again."

"Get him back," Darren Duke says. "We need him."

Kaden will be part of this . . . What do I think of that? Then I remember. The prom with Nick.

All night I want to text Kate and ask her what I should do.

My anger is fueled by my frustration. Why can't she understand that I'm trying to help her? And yet with some space since the last time we talked, I can see how wrong my approach was. I'm judging her—I know I am. And I don't know how to stop.

I can't remember the last time we didn't talk for more than two days. This time it's been three, and I wonder if she's missing me too.

While I'm working on homework, Mac comes to my room carrying the telephone.

"It's Dad," he says, pushing the phone toward my face.

"Hey, sweetie," Dad says, and hearing his voice while sitting in my room is a strange juxtaposition. "I was making plans for the weekend. I want to take you to dinner one night or out to lunch. The dance is on Saturday, right?"

"Well, maybe. I'm not sure I'm going."

"Not sure you're going to the dance?"

"Not sure I'm coming to Cottonwood."

Dad is quiet, then says with disappointment in his voice, "Okay. Well, figure it out and let me know soon, okay?"

"Okay, Dad."

I flop backward on my bed. I hate my life.

As in, I really hate it.

Anger wraps around me as I close my eyes a moment. During the divorce, and when he first was single, Dad often canceled plans with me. Mom even called to ask him to do something with me several times. Carson told me that later on. I didn't hold that against Dad; at least I don't think I did. But now I feel guilty, and it just isn't fair.

The prom is this weekend. I should be deciding on my dress—Nick keeps asking me about the color—picking out shoes, figuring out my hair. But it sounds so pointless compared to this new opportunity.

Hours ago I was happy; suddenly I'm miserable.

I can't sleep, and the weight of the world is heavy upon me. It's that familiar fog pressing in, closing off the good that I know is out there. I could write a gratitude list and go on for several pages. My mind knows of these good things, but right now none of them matters a whole lot.

When life is great, I tell myself to remember those feelings, to promise when I'm down to remember that it'll pass soon enough. But now that it's here, I can't find that feeling or those promises.

Strangely, I miss my mom, even though she's right down-stairs. Before she married Austin, I could sleep with her when I was sad or worried or upset about something. For a while part of me *liked* that she and my dad were divorced. One weekend it was just her and me—the boys were with Dad. We watched movies and ate our favorite junk foods. I wanted to get an apart-ment with just her and me.

So even with her downstairs, I miss Mom. Like I miss my dad. But the missing is for more than that. I miss my dad with my mom. I miss them together.

I want to talk to someone about this. I don't have a long enough history with Frankie and London for them to understand. Kate understands me as no one else can. But now we're not even really friends. Yeah, it's sort of immature to think childhood promises should be kept, or even can be. We said we'd be best friends forever. We'd go to college, maybe in Paris. We'd marry twin brothers and be neighbors. So okay, some of those plans were little-girl dreams, but the core of it, the meaning, was fully there. The commitment and promise to be there for one another. To never doubt that in this great big world, we at least had each other.

A feeling of anger, even hate, comes over me. How could Kate do this to me?

The walls of my room close around me. Downstairs Mac is too happy for me to be around. Mom is banging around in the kitchen. A bath sounds bad; nothing soothes me. I want this feeling to go.

But instead, when I return to my room, I see the picture that might be Aunt Betty, and I wonder about her life before she became a quirky old lady. She must have loved before Herbert, and I've never thought to even ask. Then I think of Tony, dying in his bedroom with his family sleeping through it. I remember how we loved how small he was, but surely how he hated that. He was cute Little Tony. Maybe he hated playing the Little Drummer Boy in the Christmas play.

He's dead now. I'm alive.

While I put on a movie to escape all of this, I think of Tony buried in the ground for as long as I've been living here. Proms, opportunities, divorces, and fighting with friends—none of it matters to Tony now.

The next morning I find Mom making tea.

"You're up early," she says.

"I have a dilemma." And so I tell her. But she gets immediately excited about film group.

"This is an amazing opportunity, Ruby. And besides, I thought you didn't like Nick."

"I didn't until I saw him again. And now that I'm home, I don't know again."

Mom shakes her head with a smile, as she often does. "I can't keep up with you."

"It's my job to keep you on your toes."

"More like give me more gray hairs for my hairdresser to hide." She sits on the edge of a bar stool. "You probably expect me to say this, but to me there's no choice here. Your dad will understand that you have this chance, and it's not very long at all till you'll go to Cottonwood again."

"He was excited about seeing me this weekend."

"Would it help if I called and explained it to him?"

"*Would* you call and explain it to him?"

"He'd take it better from you, but I will if you really need me to."

"I'll think about it. But if our group wins, then I'll be gone part of the summer too. Dad wants to take me camping a bunch, and I'm supposed to stay two weeks with Kate. At least that was the plan before . . ."

"Listen, it's very important to have a good relationship with both of your parents. You do need to see your dad more, just as I need to see Carson. But I'm pretty sure you'll regret it if you miss being part of this. I see how this film group has helped you adjust here and given you direction. Austin and I were just talking about it last night."

Last night I was wallowing in self-pity and pretty much every bad emotion a human can have. Remembering that, I wonder what was wrong with me.

Mom pours milk and sugar into a cup, then adds the tea from the teapot. "I'd hate to see you quit your art—which just so happens to be a pattern in your life. But then, it's hard dumping Nick, even if he only asked you a few days ago."

"I know. One of my New Year's resolutions was to stay committed to my dreams and goals. So this is like the big test. It's just hard to tell Nick. And Dad."

"I know, sweetie. And it's your decision, but you have to choose." Then Mom tries hard to hide her smile. "But one bit of advice . . . I wouldn't tell Grandma Hazel. She still thinks movies are of the devil."

This makes me chuckle. "Grandma Hazel thinks most everything is of the devil."

Then Mom feels bad for saying that, as usual, and off she goes telling the good points of her former mother-in-law, her example of faithfulness, and on and on.

But all I can think about is how I'm going to tell Nick that his second prom date is dumping him.

chapter twenty-one

I know what I have to do, but I really, really, really don't want to do it.

The coffeehouse is abuzz with the sounds of the steamer hissing away, cups chinking onto saucers, and people chatting. I make espresso drinks like second nature now and greet customers with familiar faces as my hands move to the shots of espresso, steaming milk, flavorings, and whipped topping. But underneath my outward friendliness, a nagging feeling follows me. I'll forget it for a short time, especially when a few people from school come in and I overhear them talking about Film Night.

"Can you imagine getting to spend a week this summer working on location at a real film?"

The imaginings fill my head, but then I remember Nick like a bolt of lightning zapping my chest.

Couldn't I get someone else to tell him? Kate would be the logical choice—Kate would even do it. She'd forewarn him at least, take the pressure off of me, give the poor guy a bit of notice before the blow.

On my break, I send her a text in my little attempt to smooth things out.

"Hi" is all I write.

But she doesn't respond, which angers me.

Natasha comes in with her worn leather satchel and points to her table—her signal that whenever I have time, could I bring her a tea and scone. I'm helping a few junior high–aged kids who are addicted to coffee—which is disturbing, in my opinion. They order mochas with extra shots and talk and laugh louder than I think they should. I nod to Natasha.

Awhile later I carry her Chai tea with an extra teaspoon of Mexican vanilla—an experiment I'm trying.

She takes a sip and smiles. "This is really quite good, Ruby. You may have created a new favorite for me."

The people who come to the Underground are the best part of my job. Some happiness rises in me to see the old guys at their tables. There are some customers passing through the area, and I love to hear where they're going. The stories I get from them are enough for a hundred films. But Natasha is by far my favorite.

Later I catch a glimpse of her at her table, sitting with her pile of books and tea. I wonder about her. About what she does for fun, if she's lonely at night and missing her husband, about all those little daily rituals, friendships, family connections, and interests that create a person's life.

She waves at me, and I come over with a dish towel in my hand.

"You and I need to sit down for a cup of tea sometime."

"I was just thinking how I'd love to join you."

"Did you have your break already?"

"No, I haven't," I say.

"Great then. I plan to be here a few hours."

I clean a table near her, stacking the dishes and carrying them into the kitchen.

"So when do you leave for your trip?" I ask when I return to wash the small oval table.

"I still have a few months to go."

"I bet you can't wait."

"Well, part of me can. I have a lot to do, and strangely, it's as much fun preparing as it is going. The hardest part used to be the post-trip depression. But now I've even eliminated that."

"How did you do that?"

"I've learned to discipline my thoughts—and to look at my life from different perspectives."

"Huh?" I ask. A few customers walk in; I look at them and then back at Natasha. "I'll come back."

After a while Aunt Jenna tells me to go on my break, so I bring a maple scone and a Kenya-blend coffee and sit with Natasha. She stacks her books onto another empty chair and smiles as I sit down.

We talk about travel and favorite books, and then I go back to her earlier subject. "What did you mean about looking at life from other perspectives?"

Natasha smiles, and the lines around her bright blue eyes deepen.

"Every day, understandably, we see the things that encompass our lives from our own perspective. But feelings, opinions, our age, moods, our past, to name a few things, cloud the truth of what really is."

"I get that."

"When we see beyond our perspective to what really is and also see other people's view, we come a long way in understanding truth and other people."

Kate comes to mind. And I realize I haven't thought about her perspective. What would it be like to be the one left behind? Kate has a lot of friends, but nothing like our friendship. And then she meets this guy she really likes, and immediately I'm against it.

"And what did you mean by disciplining your thoughts? I'm not sure I'd want to. I love making up stories as I go through the day."

"Oh, I'm a definite supporter of imagination. I'm referring to those harmful rebel thoughts and feelings that need to be put in their proper place. For instance, after my husband died, I couldn't get out of living in the past. I kept thinking about the past, being angry that we didn't get to do half of the things we'd dreamed of doing together. It consumed me. Then a friend challenged me not to allow those thoughts in. That seemed impossible, but I decided to let myself be sad on the fifteenth of every month. Whenever I was sad, I'd tell myself to stop it, that on the fifteenth I'd be sad all day long."

"But I bet on the fifteenth you didn't want to be sad."

"Sometimes I did. But usually I was okay, even on the fifteenth. I miss my husband every day. I miss our dreams and just his presence in the house, even watching TV together. But I don't let it control my thoughts and emotions. I take the love for him with me everywhere, and that makes me happy instead of depressed."

Natasha is quiet a moment, sipping her tea and staring into the liquid like it's a fortune-teller's crystal ball. Maybe she'll tell me exactly how to solve my future.

"Time doesn't get slower, I promise you that. There are many ways to go, many opportunities, and exciting things to do. I want to see every country in the world. I want a thousand things, and I could fill my life with obsessive pursuit of them. But that wouldn't fulfill me, give my life meaning or purpose."

Something in the words *meaning* and *purpose* reverberates through me like the beat of bass through a woofer. They are what I've wanted for as long as I can remember. Yet I haven't thought much about my life having meaning or a purpose in a while. Since moving here, my thoughts have been mostly about me, and the things I want, and the things that interest me. Even my friendship with Kate has been more about her supporting me, and she's the one who needs the support.

"Ruby, I wish I could give you the key to life's answers. But what I know is this. Seek God for what to do in your life. Seek God to know meaning and to know Him. Ask Him to guide you into who He wants you to be."

"But how do you know when God is telling you something?"

"When I'm trying to decide where to go in the world next, I spin the globe with my eyes shut and stop it spinning some-place—"

Natasha laughs then as she sees my incredulous look.

"I'm kidding. Well, okay, sometimes I do that for fun. But to hear God, I always have to listen carefully while I'm seeking Him. You seek God by just talking to Him with your open and honest heart. And then you listen."

"The small, still voice—there's a verse about that, I think."

"Some say it's your own intuition, your inner self speaking. But I don't agree."

"Why not?"

"It's important to pay attention to the intuition and common sense God gave us. But I think if someone is truly seeking God, the one true God who created love and life, and they listen in the stillness, God will speak. So follow that quiet voice."

Later that night, I prop myself up in bed and reach for my journal. I've been thinking all day about my conversation with Natasha. I write "Finding God's Purpose" at the top of a page, and underneath I write questions as fast as I think of them: "What am I drawn to? Is it good for me? Am I talented at it? What gets in the way of my doing it? Am I listening for the small, still voice?"

I wonder how many other people are like me. Most of my friends back home don't write out goals or God's-purpose lists. They appear content to just live, be in their clubs, play sports and train, and focus on getting good grades to get into good colleges to get good jobs. But my brain won't stop there. I need meaning. I want to do something special and be someone special. Is that wrong?

My phone beeps in the middle of these thoughts. I can't resist looking to see who sent a text.

Nick.

Regret comes quickly. I meant to call him earlier.

NICK: So have you picked our colors yet? My mom wants
    to get my tie tomorrow.

Is it cowardly to do this through a text message? Yes, it's totally cowardly.

NICK: And do you want a wrist corsage or one that pins
    to your dress. My mom thought the wrist one so it
    doesn't mess up your dress.

I should call him. I should dial his number right now.

ME: Nick.
NICK: Yeah?
ME: I can't come.
NICK: Ha-ha.

I drop the phone on my lap and stare at the one piece of artwork I've hung in my room. A poster of a Salvador Dali painting. In the painting, the artist painted himself painting, but he's also staring out from the canvas and extending a hand as if to seek a hand of help to pull him from the canvas. Though right now, I think maybe he's actually offering a hand, reaching out, and if only I could grasp it, he'd pull me away from all this and into the surrealistic world of the painting.

Ah, yes, *perspective*. I need to think of Nick and not put this off any longer.

My phone buzzes again.

NICK: You're kidding, right? Tell me you're kidding.

ME: Wish I was. I'm really sorry.

NICK: Wait, no. You have to come.

ME: It's a long story, but I really can't come.

NICK: Uh. K.

ME: Do you think you can find someone else?

NICK: Now? It was a stretch for you to say yes. But then it worked out with Nikki. She would've gone with me and . . .

ME: I'm so so sorry. What can I do?

NICK: Come be my date.

chapter twenty-two

"So he probably hates me," I say to Mom. It's a few minutes before time to leave for school. I didn't sleep well again, and when I did, my head was full of strange dreams, both good and bad.

Mom and I stand in the kitchen eating cereal and drinking coffee.

"He won't go alone or in a group?" Mom asks as she chews her organic, cardboardy-looking oat bran cereal.

"What guy would? Not the jock kind anyway."

"I meant to remind you to call him yesterday. The opportunity with your film group sort of blinded my parental judgment, and then I had that article due last night. I do wonder whether it's right to ruin Nick's prom because something better came along. You did give him your word."

"But you said I should—"

"I know. But if he can't find a date, we really should keep your commitment to him."

"Then I'd miss the main work weekend on the film. They may not let me stay in the group if I'm not here."

"Yes, I know. And I was going to tell you that your group could have the work weekend here," Mom says. "Austin and I will hardly be here this weekend. We're meeting your dad partway to drop Mac, then to pick him up."

"I heard my name," Mac says, walking into the kitchen with his backpack on over his pajamas.

"We could hang out upstairs, or if everything looked okay, maybe we'd spend the weekend in the garage apartment . . ." She's mumbling to herself as she plans it out, then returns to our discussion. "There would be no drinking or drugs or anything going on, right?"

"Like she'd tell you," Mac says and laughs at himself for being so clever.

"It's an intense work weekend. I can't imagine Rob allowing any sort of partying. There'll be coffee, Monsters, and Red Bulls, I'm sure."

"Let me talk to Austin, but you first need to figure out the prom. I know what I'd like for you, but I want you to do the right thing too."

But what is the right thing to do? I wonder. Mom isn't being very helpful in this.

On the way to school, I get a text from Jeffers.

> JEFFERS: Wow, you aren't the favorite person in
> Cottonwood right now.

ME: So everyone hates me?

JEFFERS: I didn't say that.

ME: Nick probably does. Though I'm still going to be his
     date if he can't find someone else.

JEFFERS: Okay, I admit this to you and you alone. Nick is
     one of my best friends, but let's face it, that ego of his
     can get a bit too big for a head that's not that great.

ME: Nick has an ego?

JEFFERS: He hides it well, I'll give him that. But in sports,
     he's gotta be the best or else it's excuses as to why
     he's not. And why hasn't he had a girlfriend before?
     Is it because he's shy, or can't make up his mind, or
     is intimidated by smart women like you—oh no. He's
     a tightwad and doesn't want the work of a girlfriend.
     Now it's like some kind of monster has been
     unleashed. He'll be a player in college, I can see it
     already.

ME: I still feel bad leaving him without a date.

JEFFERS: Yeah, but you really shouldn't. He's going with
     Jackie.

ME: He is! He didn't even tell me.

Funny how offended I am that he's replaced me so quickly.
And yet this should be a relief—an answer to prayer if I'd prayed.
It is a relief too, but another part of me wanted to see my friends
and maybe make up with Kate.

JEFFERS: That guy needs to be dumped. All this drama
     around him is making him really hard to be around.

ME: What's Kate say about all this?

JEFFERS: She isn't saying much. Everyone knows the two
of you had a fight. But it's understandable.

ME: Why do you say that?

JEFFERS: Sometimes we gotta say things that our friends
don't like. That's what a true friend is.

ME: So you think what she said was right?

JEFFERS: What she said to you? Huh, what? I'm confused.
I heard that you didn't like her having a grown man
as her boyfriend.

ME: Everyone knows about that? I thought he was a
secret.

JEFFERS: Did you move to Mars? Of course everyone
knows. Didn't you know her parents caught her at
his apartment? She's grounded for like forever. I
think till she's thirty or something.

ME: No way!

I immediately send a note to Kate.

ME TO KATE: I heard what happened? Are you okay?

An auto-response comes back to me:

Kate is unavailable at this time and for the near future.

ME TO JEFFERS: No way!!!! I just tried writing her.

JEFFERS: I don't want any of my friends dating some
college guy. She's too naive. He probably took
advantage of that. He did, didn't he?

ME: I told her she was naive too. And I don't know
    anything else.
JEFFERS: That means he did.
ME: No, it doesn't.
JEFFERS: So they didn't.
ME: Didn't?
JEFFERS: So they DID! I knew it! We'll kill him.
ME: Wait, stop, no!
JEFFERS: No?
ME: What do I know, we had a fight, remember?

So it's a bit of another lie, but Jeffers doesn't need to know something that personal, and shouldn't even ask. Jeffers would spread it all over the school in the excuse of protecting her.

My friend needs me. And I'm hundreds of miles and quite a few commitments away.

He stares into the book like he's searching into a deep well trying to find something. I don't interrupt him but instead sit beside Josef on the other end of the table with my heart doing such a tuck and roll that the breath I take sounds more like a gasp. Josef glances up at me like maybe I saw a ghost, but I act like nothing is wrong, say hello, and pull out a notebook from my book bag.

Kaden hasn't looked up.

He said he'd e-mail me, but he didn't. Rob mentioned family trouble, and I wonder what that was about. A family death, mother with cancer, car accident?

I've tried to forget Kaden, be angry at him, but seeing him at the other end of the table, immersed in a thick book, I'm surprised again by the attraction I feel.

His dark lashes remain angled downward as he turns the page. What is he reading? His hands draw my attention next; long, thin fingers hold the book, and his pinky finger looks a little crooked, like my right pinky. People are chatting around us, but Kaden is lost in the world of the pages.

A static noise makes me look around. "Starship to Ruby, are you out there, Ruby?"

Josef's voice sounds exactly like a Starfleet commander over an intercom. It makes me laugh.

"Sorry, were you saying something?"

"I asked you on a date?"

"What?" My mouth drops.

"You don't have to look so horrified. I was kidding."

"Oh, sorry. I was thinking about something."

"Uh-huh," he says and glances over at Kaden at the other end of the table.

"What?" I say as innocently as possible, but a small smile creeps up the edges of my lips. Why can't I control that evil little traitor smile? It always gives me away.

Rob comes to the rescue when he arrives and pulls out his PDA and starts tapping it with the stylus. "Let's get started, people. I know several of us have the awards banquet at the Raphael Center, so let's make this quick."

And the meeting is quick. It establishes the team expectations, a schedule, and the announcement that the work weekend will be held at my house, which brings all eyes toward me.

I notice Kaden's linger on me a long while as the group breaks up. I've avoided his eyes all through the meeting, knowing he glanced my way a number of times. And yet isn't this the biggest indicator that there is something abnormal with all this forced and overemphasized normality?

As I bend under the table to retrieve a book that slid from my book bag, I hear, "Hey."

I recognize that voice, though in all actuality, I haven't heard it all that much. He sets a paper on the table that says "Top 100 Movies."

"Always handing me papers," I say and hope he doesn't see my hands shaking. What's come over me?

"Really? Oh yes, the film group flyer." He smiles, and my eyes linger on his lips. "Yeah, I meant to e-mail it, but I went out of town for a while."

"That's okay," I say as if I don't care.

"I have to tell you, I don't really talk much."

"Okay."

"I mean online or on the phone. So if that's something you like, I'm just telling you now."

I stare at him. What does that even mean?

"Okay."

He's kind of weird. So why do I like him so much?

Kaden motions to the paper.

Dang, he does have a Johnny Depp thing going on.

"I put stars by the movies I watched and gave them ratings. Five stars is highest."

Looking at the paper, some of the movies have two to four stars. Only a few have five.

"Nice," I say and find it enormously cute that he went to so much work. "I'll be tempted to watch the five-star ones first."

"Don't give in to that temptation. Watch as many as possible and give them your own rating. After you watch about ten movies, let's compare thoughts."

"Okay," I say, then wonder if that would be something like a date. Before I decide whether to jokingly ask this, his phone rings to a tune by Bon Jovi.

He looks at the number and says abruptly, "Guess I'll see you this weekend then. Bye."

And once again I'm watching Kaden walk away.

chapter twenty-three

Kate, are you okay?

I send the message not from my phone but by thought, out to the air, concentrating in the way she and I did when we were little and determined to be telepathic—or rather, I was determined, and Kate always went along with my wildly creative ideas. One of us would write down what she was thinking; then the other would press her fingers to her forehead and concentrate. I remember it worked only once, and that might have been because we were smelling Mom's homemade pizza. When I guessed *food* and Kate had written down *pizza*, we believed we'd come far in our quest of ESP.

Kate, stop ignoring me!

I'll ignore you if I want to.

My head perks up.

I'm worried about you.

You should be.

Are you okay?

Pizza.

This is when I wake up. Immediately I reach for my phone, and for about the tenth time send Kate a text. Immediately there's a response:

Kate is unavailable at this time. Thank you, Kate's Mom

I stare out the balcony door where only a bit of light comes through. The fog must be thick and hiding even the streetlights. All week I've tried convincing Mom to call Kate's mom and find out how they're all doing. She says that's nosy and will appear that she's fishing for info. But she would be fishing for info! It's a constant annoying itch for me not to know what's happening or if Kate is okay. This is one of the worst things to happen to my friend. Is she heartbroken? Angry? Sad? Lonely?

My other friends aren't giving me much information either. They've been consumed with prom planning and hardly any have seen or talked to Kate.

I might as well stick with telepathy.

On Friday when I arrive home from school, I walk in the door to a very clean house and voices I don't recognize in the kitchen.

Cass and Darren Duke sit on bar stools around the island, eating chocolate chip cookies and drinking milk.

"Look what your mom made us," Darren Duke says with a smile that makes me suddenly imagine him as an eight-year-old with freckles on his nose.

Mom is putting dishes into the dishwasher. "I made lasagna and salad—they're in the fridge. There's French bread, and I bought some snacks that are in the pantry. And yes, I made the lasagna, not Austin," she clarifies to me.

"The last homemade lasagna I ate was when my grandmother was alive. My dad isn't much of a cook," Cass says as she dips her cookie in the milk. They both look strangely young and unsophisticated in my mother's kitchen.

Darren Duke makes a long *Mmm* sound with another bite. "I swear this is the best cookie I've eaten in my life. I'll just get all my belongings and move into the basement, if that's okay?"

Mom laughs, and I'm still standing in the doorway with my bag weighing down my shoulder. I look from one to the other—Mom with Cass and Darren Duke. This scene is pretty weird.

So Mom cleaned all day, brought out sleeping bags, baked a huge pile of her chocolate chip cookies and dinner for one night, and she welcomes the first film group arrivals like they've come for my tenth birthday party.

Mac's voice drifts up from the basement, and I wonder who else is here. A few minutes later he and Kaden come walking up the stairs, chatting like old war buddies.

"Cool house. And cool little brother," he says as they pass me, and Mac beams a wide smile and shrugs his shoulders.

A shiver of something goes through me as Kaden nearly brushes my shoulder. I'm not sure what the something is; it's new and surprising and completely . . . well, disconcerting.

"Just wait till you get to know him," I say in an awkward tone that doesn't sound like me. "I've watched two of the movies on the list—"

"Hey, Mac." Austin's voice from upstairs interrupts me. He comes down the stairs, carrying a duffel bag in each hand and a toiletry bag under his arm. "Hey, Mac, come give me a hand. Hi there, Kaden."

"I'll help," Kaden says.

He takes a duffel from Austin as Mac dramatically takes the small toiletry bag as if it weighs a hundred pounds. They head off to the apartment over the garage. I'm still standing there with my book bag on my shoulder.

An hour later Mom, Austin, and Mac are gone to meet Dad, and the equipment and team members are still coming in.

"Time to work." Darren Duke opens his laptop bag on the coffee table.

Rob assesses the rooms, going down to the basement and back to where eight of us now wait. I'm surprised and relieved to find that Blair isn't coming. Her part in the production is over.

Rob says, "We'll make workstations here and in the basement. We've got food and drinks for tonight, and tomorrow we'll get something delivered. We can get a lot done by staying focused, everyone working hard. We shouldn't have trouble getting this nearly done, then next week we'll polish, and Thursday is the big day. So consider us locked in for now."

Equipment is set up in the living room, and the basement is transformed into an editing room. Rob is pleased with the acoustics and layout of the basement.

The members settle into their places, and I corner Rob in the kitchen as he's eating a cookie.

"I'm not even sure what to do. I don't want to get in the way, but I definitely want to help."

"Yeah, I was going to come talk to you—man, these are good cookies." He takes another bite. "If you don't mind just sort of roving to different people who need your help, since you're still new to all this. We might do a few reshoots in the yard—that flower garden will be perfect. Try to gain as much knowledge as you can. It'll be like a crash course in filmmaking."

"Sounds great."

For some reason I find myself avoiding Kaden. His presence is too unsettling. And so for most of the evening I sit with Sound Guy and learn about the different sound effects and intensities.

Frankie writes me as I'm doing dishes after dinner.

FRANKIE: Are you slaving away?

ME: Just call me Helper Girl.

FRANKIE: Would you pick me up some toothpaste and coffee creamer, Helper Girl?

ME: It would help if I had my driver's license.

FRANKIE: Yeah, it's like Batman without his cape.

ME: You mean Superman without his cape.

FRANKIE: Batman has a cape.

ME: But it's not really used for anything except looking cool when it swooshes around him.

FRANKIE: That's what I mean. Batman wouldn't be so cool without his swooshing cape. It's a necessary item for him.

ME: But Superman really needs his cape, to actually fly. Like I need a car to actually do the errands.

FRANKIE: Want me to bring my little Lexus cape and fly you around?

ME: I'm in the middle of dishes so guess I'm also
   Cleaning Girl.

FRANKIE: The oh so many sides of Ruby Blue. But I have
   a night out, so I'll leave you to your cleaning.

ME: BNNF

FRANKIE: You know I could come up with obscene things
   for every little abbreviation.

ME: BYE NOW, NOT FOREVER

FRANKIE: Got it. BNNFTGRZPXI

ME: I'm not even going to ask.

FRANKIE: Smart Girl.

Our film *Solitude* will be twenty minutes long. There are storyboard images on a giant corkboard in the living room depicting the essential scenes. The night is like a mosaic of happenings, conversations, and little work groups that compose the larger image of our group at work to bring those scenes to life, to make the sound perfect and the colors vivid or muted depending on the effect, and to create something that enters the viewers' eyes, to move through their heads and emotions and remain in their memories.

I love hearing the group talk about the different angles, tightening a scene, the technical words and directions that I don't quite understand. And then just the chatter about movies that are loved, movie moments that shocked, scared, and inspired.

"When Bruce Willis discovers he's dead in *The Sixth Sense*."

"*Kill Bill 2* when Uma rips out Darrel Hannah's one remaining eye."

"Tarantino is master."

"Tarantino has some serious issues."

"*Amelie* with the father getting postcards from his traveling gnome from around the world."

Then someone asks, "Ruby, what's one of your favorite movie moments?"

"The scene in *Shawshank Redemption* when Tim Robbins escapes prison and rises from the sewer into the rain."

Everyone nods and says, "Ah, yes." As if this moment is reverent.

"If we could get something of the buildup to that scene in *Shawshank Redemption* . . . Let's look at the three scenes before the climax again," Rob says, and they're off into creation mode again. And it's nice that twice now I've incited conversation from answering a film question, instead of ridicule.

Rob has me shadow everyone at one time or another. It's interesting seeing the many stages and intricate details. Rob encourages everyone to learn each part of the movie production.

When I sit with Kaden in the basement to see what he's doing, that familiar nervousness flutters through me. *Keep calm, Ruby,* I keep telling myself.

"My job is to go through each scene from the storyboard," Kaden says, showing me the sketches on the massive board that depict each scene. "I'm building the rough cut from the scenes, choosing the best takes if Rob hasn't already, and sometimes changing the order of the best shots. From there we'll work on the final cut, where we make sure all the shots flow smoothly into one seamless story. Sometimes just shaving off a few seconds or a bit of unnecessary dialogue can make a scene stronger. Did you ever see the movie *Meet Joe Black* with Brad Pitt?"

"Yeah, I liked that movie."

"I did too, but not many people would agree. The editing wasn't tight. The film dragged. If they'd have cut ten minutes off that film, the flow and tension would've been greatly heightened."

"Interesting."

"I'll show you some examples."

Kaden shows me two identical sections of the film. I can't really see the difference, but I like the first one better for some reason. We watch the two versions several more times until I see it. He shortened part of the dialogue and cut a moment of camera sweeping over the landscape.

"I liked seeing the landscape though," I say. "It was a beautiful shot of the city."

"Yeah, I liked it too. But it's better, cleaner, with that part gone. Film editing is similar to writing. We should 'kill our darlings,' as they say. If the story is best served without it, then it goes."

"And this is better, though I don't know why."

"By taking out the clutter, the next scene becomes more precise. The viewer has fewer images in her head, and so the scene that is important, the image of the doorway to the courtyard with the boy standing there, impacts us more."

"Less is more, as they say."

"Exactly. Though sometimes clutter and 'more' is what the film needs—but this is rare."

"Like when?"

"Um, well, let's say there's a man and woman, and a romantic tension is built between them. Like in *Mr. and Mrs. Smith.* There's all this fighting and shooting; they destroy their house trying to kill each other. Then when they get close, suddenly they kiss. The intensity suddenly halts. So it's like the opposite effect. High intensity and then a frozen moment. Or low building up into a cataclysmic climax—both of them can be very effective ways to complete a film."

And then Kaden pauses, looking at me with such gentle intensity—a mixture of both methods he just talked about, and he doesn't even realize the degree of his effect. It surprises even me.

I wake up thirsty, sitting in a chair at three in the morning, and find most of the crew asleep upright in chairs around me. Sound Guy is on the floor with his head on a duffel bag. Empty plates and half-empty cups cover the coffee table, and I have to step around sleeping bags, cords, and a giant bag of Doritos. As I walk up the stairs, the flash of the TV in the living room lights my way. Cass and Olivia are asleep on the couch and love seat.

In the kitchen, Kaden leans close to the computer screen with his fist curled and resting against his forehead. Black ear-buds, jeans, sweatshirt, dark hair slightly messed up, and six empty Red Bulls are lined up in front of him.

"Too wired to sleep?" I open the refrigerator and pull out the lasagna and a sparkling water and set them on the countertop.

"I like working at night actually."

"Do you want to be left alone?"

"Naw, but I'll have some cold lasagna." He smiles.

I get two forks and we eat it from the pan. "How's it going?" I ask, motioning to the computer.

"I think I'm done with the timing and editing of the first two acts. But sometimes what I think after a late night of Red Bulls isn't what I think in the light of morning. This house is peaceful at night. And you know, you have a really nice family."

"Yeah, they're okay."

Kaden leans back in his chair and looks at me for a long time.

I shift awkwardly. What does he see when he looks at me? Does he like what he finds or notice my flaws like the small scar above my right eyebrow?

"It's hard to be grateful for things that are normal to us," he says.

I nod but don't quite know what he means. "Yeah, that's true."

"I saw you at church once," Kaden says, returning his eyes to the screen.

"We're trying different ones. I didn't see you."

"Was late and left early. My mom used to be really involved in church."

I wonder how one is related to the other.

"A few years ago my family was pretty involved at church," I say. "My parents were children's church coordinators."

"So you aren't so involved now because of the divorce?"

"Um, sort of, I guess. I still go to youth group and to church sometimes. Well, I did at home."

"Do you blame your wavering faith on your parents' divorce?"

"Who says I have wavering faith?"

"I thought you did."

"I didn't say that." I go over what we've just said, and I *know* I didn't say anything about my faith. What presumptions he makes. "Are you always this, this . . ."

"What?"

"Nothing."

"No, really, tell me." He smiles slightly. "I want to know."

"Confrontational. Abrupt."

He's smiling instead of being offended, and this wide smile is such an offset to his usual serious expression that it makes me smile as well. With my defenses down, I realize that Kaden is right even without my saying it. My faith has waned; it may only barely exist. Is that what he saw with his prodding eyes?

"What else am I?" he asks, chuckling.

"Weird."

He's laughing now. "Weird as in how? Give me examples."

"Really?"

"Yes, tell me. I like hearing these things, 'cause I know I need to change some oddities I've acquired."

"Well . . . weird like when you handed me that flyer at school. No explanation, no talking much at all. You don't say hello or good-bye; you hardly ever do. There's, like, no small talk with you. It's straight to the point and then it's over and you're gone."

"See? I need to hear these things, even if they hurt." Kaden puts a hand over his heart like he's been shot, but with the same small grin on his face.

"I'm sorry."

"You say 'sorry' a lot—do you realize that?"

"I do?"

"You say sorry for things you shouldn't be sorry for."

"Hmm."

"But at least you aren't weird."

This makes him chuckle, and I nearly apologize again when I realize maybe "I'm sorry" is an auto-response I speak more than I realize.

"You know what's really weird is that I was a really happy kid. People always said that about me—what a happy and friendly boy I was."

"You?"

"Yeah, I know. Your little brother reminds me of myself— well, the old me. My social skills have gotten pretty rusty. I'm better with kids and the elderly now."

I push the lasagna pan closer to Kaden and find a Ziploc bag of chocolate chip cookies in the bread box. "You keep saying *now*. What's that about?"

"There's the before and the after—or the then and the now." The smile remains, but sadness falls through his features like a curtain dropping.

I hand Kaden two cookies and sit on the bar stool next to him. The hum of the refrigerator is the only sound beyond the two of us, our breathing and voices and movements.

"I bet it's like that for you and your brothers. There's the before the divorce. And then the now."

I nod slowly. "Yeah. It's like some tragedy or something that changed us all, and yet we're all still here. There wasn't a funeral or any single event to be sad about. I think there should be a funeral when families die. It might make it easier. Did your parents get a divorce?"

"No. Not a divorce."

I don't know if I should ask, and then I just do. "So what did happen to make the before and the now?"

He nods as if to himself, as if knowing I'd ask and that if I did, he'd answer. "You really want to hear this story?"

I nod.

"Okay, well, where to start?" He rubs his forehead and pinches the skin between his eyes. "In eighth grade I was having trouble in school. There was this bully and this girl—but that's another story. Anyway, my parents were fighting a lot. I know they talked about divorce. And then they were being dragged to my school because of my sudden drop in grades and this big fight I started."

"You? A fighter?"

"Yeah, sometimes I can be. But it was to defend this girl, but—"

"That's another story," I say, which makes him smile and nod.

"So at home, the fighting between my parents continued and was really affecting me. I was angry all the time, and so I had to see the school counselor.

"Then, almost overnight, my parents stopped fighting. My dad wasn't home very much, but he promised it was for a short time. He brought my mom flowers every single night for two weeks. The house was so full of flowers that my older brother had a major allergy attack. Then Dad surprised us with a vacation snowboarding in Canada. He hadn't taken us on vacation in years. It was the only family trip I could remember since I was pretty young. And during the trip, my dad went all-out, which wasn't like him. We ate at expensive restaurants, bought souvenirs, went boarding five days in a row. And he bought us each a gift to remember the trip by.

"Then we came home, and a week later my father killed himself."

"Oh," I hear myself gasp. My mind replays the words *killed himself* as if to really believe it's what Kaden said.

"No one knew he'd killed himself at first. It looked like an accident. His car went off a cliff. This highway patrol officer came to the house and told us. It was a minimum day at school, and Mom and I were looking at pictures she'd printed out of our trip. She wanted my opinion on which picture to use for our Christmas cards."

"Oh," I say again.

"You think things can't get any worse after something like that. Then a few days later my mom got a letter from Dad in the mail. His suicide note. He told her not to let anyone see the note because the insurance company wouldn't pay the life insurance."

He's quiet for so long, staring down at his hands, that I worry I've upset him. "You don't have to tell me any of this, you know."

"The note said how much he loved us. That he'd made a lot of really bad mistakes in his life, but it wasn't my mom's fault or mine or my brother's. He said he knew it wasn't right to kill himself—but he felt it was the right thing to do for us. For us— isn't that crazy?"

Kaden looks at me then. His jaw clenches and releases. "My dad thought we'd be better off without him. Later Mom found out about some illegal things he'd been doing at work, and about some other women in his life. She hasn't really told me a lot of that, and I haven't asked."

"I'm so sorry, Kaden."

"In, like, one week, our dad was gone, everyone was there, supporting us, helping us out, and then my mom told us about the letter. She let us read it, saying that we were old enough to know the truth. Then she called and told the insurance company. We talked about keeping his suicide a secret from our friends and family, but before we made any family decision, someone found out, and everything changed. People acted weird around us, and we had several families come over who were also 'suicide families,' and we had to hear their sob stories. My brother dropped out of college to work; then we moved here when Mom got a job at a mortgage company and we moved in with my uncle."

"If you had gotten it, how much was the insurance for?"

"Two million dollars."

"Wow. You gotta admire your mom for that one."

"At first I didn't. I was so angry." He pauses a moment. "I've never told this to anyone. Not anyone."

"I'll never tell."

"I'm not trying to keep it a secret. And maybe it's easier talking to you because I've talked with your family. They told me so much about you that I felt like I knew you before we met."

He takes a slow, thoughtful bite of the cookie, and I hold back my questions about what exactly my family said about me.

"I don't care if people know about my dad, as long as they don't pity me."

"I can understand that. Rob said you were gone a lot last month because of family stuff."

"Family stuff, huh?" he says with a tired smile. "It was the two-year anniversary. We went back to Portland. My brother lives there and needed help. The three of us went to the cemetery, and he had this breakdown. They think he has some psychological problems."

"That's terrible."

"Yeah, but it doesn't really surprise me. Daniel never dealt with my dad's death. He dove into work and then into drinking. He won't admit it, but I think he's been doing some pretty serious drugs. All of that has a big effect on a sensitive soul like Daniel. But I think he's going to be okay."

"Sad."

"It is. I, on the other hand, had a lot of help. My pastor in Portland was incredible. He helped me a lot and partnered me with this guy who lost his son in a car crash. We sort of adopted each other. We still keep in touch."

"My life feels so easy compared to all this."

"You've had losses. It's important to grieve them. Makes moving on easier. I'll never 'get over' my dad, but the pain doesn't control me now. And honestly, Ruby . . ."

He thinks for a few moments, and there's comfort now in waiting for his thoughts to materialize into words. I like how he thinks long before speaking.

"Without my faith, I might be like my brother."

"But if you go away from it, how do you get back?"

"I don't know for sure. But I guess you start seeking again and again."

It's surprising how quickly Sunday comes and everything is being packed up. My house slowly looks like my house again as we pick up the equipment, empty cartons of Chinese takeout, dozens of empty aluminum cans, clothes, sleeping bags, and dishes.

And except for some minor tweaking, the film is done.

The group sits together and watches it on Kaden's laptop.

Even with my limited professional experience, I know it's good. Really good.

Kaden and I look at each other when it's over, as everyone gives high fives and congratulations. Except for Rob, who is still evaluating and writing thoughts on perfecting what to me is perfect.

I imagine Rob's father standing as the credits roll, and the entire crowd applauding so loudly it shakes the upstairs. The cast and crew are brought up to the front amid further accolades and whistles of admiration.

And this summer our team will be filming on some tropical location. Kaden and I can walk the beach at midnight. Maybe we'll swim in the warm waters beneath the moonlight. Stranger things have happened.

chapter twenty-four

After school as I wait by London's white MINI Cooper, Blair walks toward me with a cold look on her face. Even colder than usual.

And did I really think time would make this all disappear?

It's been so long, I hoped she either didn't know or didn't care. Since I dropped International Cooking for Intro to Film, I don't have lunch with Frankie and friends.

My phone vibrates, and I look at the message from Rob.

ROB: I'm sick and still working on the program, SG's grandma passed away so he's on his way to Iowa, Cass and the others are helping set up and print the brochures. I need you to pick up the final cut from SG and get it to the Underground this afternoon.

"We need to talk." Blair is standing in front of me.

"I can't right now. Rob wants me to pick up the film for tonight."

I hold up my phone as if to prove it, and she frowns.

"Soon then."

"There you are," London says. "Oh, hello, Blair."

"Bye," Blair says, giving me one last glance that reminds me this isn't finished.

"I think Blair could take down a UFC fighter with one of her looks," London says as she unlocks her car doors with a touch of her finger to the lock. "I think you deserve a short spa afternoon before the big night. My treat."

I laugh at that—it's always her treat, or I couldn't afford it. "If I didn't know better, I'd think you lived at that spa."

"It's been said before."

"I have to work a few hours before the big night begins."

"You can't work," she says with a funny little whine. "I want a spa buddy."

"And I would love to be that girl. But I have to pick up the film, go home and get my stuff, get to work, get ready, and be ready for tonight and the Pellegrini Filmmakers Competition."

"Please, stop, stop. Too much for the brain."

I laugh. For a short while after the "party night," I didn't hang out with London. She deserted me, after all, even if she did apologize again and again. But her persistence won me back. And she is fun.

"Hey, could you drive me by SG's house to pick up the film?" I ask.

"Of course, darling," she says with a British accent. "Your chauffeur at your service."

As I'm looking for the key under the doormat at the side entrance of SG's condo, Mom calls.

"Aunt Jenna asked if you could come in a little early."

"Uh, yeah, sure. We just got to SG's house. I'll grab the film, get my stuff at home, and go straight over."

"And you know that your brother can't come down? Your dad has some shipment arriving tonight for the hardware store . . ."

I unlock the door and peer inside. SG's parents moved to Washington earlier in the year and set him up with his own condo that he shares with two college students who are currently on a weeklong trek for the environment—or something like that. Stepping inside, I try to remember all the instructions he gave me when I called him on the drive over.

"Yeah, I talked to Carson on Monday or sometime."

"Your dad said to tell you good luck and that he wants to see the movie when you come up."

I go down the hall, glancing around at the decor a la bachelor. Overstuffed couch, plasma TV, and mess of pizza boxes and half-empty glasses.

"Okay. I'll try to call him soon."

"What time do you want us there?"

On a desk in one of the rooms, I see a disk with the title *Solitude* on top. I grab it and hurry back to the car.

"Mom, I'm on my way home now. Can we talk then?"

London zips down the road quickly. At home I race inside, dump out my book bag, and reload it with my makeup, shoes, curling iron, and jewelry for tonight. I nearly forget my little black dress that's become a little tight lately with all the food I've been eating. But it still complements my curving hips in a good way—not like the way some of my low-rise pants are starting to fit.

London's talking to Anthony when I get back in the car.

"To the Underground!" I say with my hand pointing forward.

When we arrive, London helps me gather my purse, duffel bag, camera, phone, and dress.

"Where's the film?" she asks.

I find the disc partway down the side of the seat. "Oh my gosh, can you imagine if something happened to this?" I say, holding it close to my chest.

Work passes at a snail's pace. I keep checking the clock. Members of my team and the other film groups arrive and go up and down to the theater rooms with little to do and anxiety exuding from every pore.

Finally I change quickly in the back room, wash my face, and redo my makeup. I decide on smoky eyes for a night like tonight, but my favorite gloss isn't in my makeup bag. I think of London's perfectly organized travel makeup "station" and smile as I dump my makeup bag out and finally find the gloss. Tossing everything in the corner under the small desk, I'm about to leave when I hear a text come in.

> KATE: I'd like to talk.
> ME: Oh yes. Me too! I can't right now though. Later
>   tonight?

KATE: Yeah.

ME: Are you okay?

She doesn't respond, and I need to find my team.

Rob isn't his normal, easygoing self. He's more like Simon from *American Idol* on steroids and with a cold—he's grouchy and constantly moving while blowing his nose occasionally.

"Ruby, meet us downstairs," he calls and disappears.

Mom, Austin, and Mac arrive. I wave and tell them I have to go. "You might want to get seats soon," I tell them before following Cass and Darren Duke to the theater rooms.

It's time. The air nearly crackles with the anticipation.

Three of the teams are seated at the back, with the one whose film is showing sitting in the front row. The leader of each will stand and offer a brief Q&A session after the showing. Our group will present third. The judges sit in a row in the middle—two other men and a woman whom people are impressed with but whom I've never heard of.

After finding a seat with my team, I lean around Cass, who is talking to someone behind her, and wave at Kaden. He's staring forward in one of his deep thought moments.

"Pretty exciting, isn't it?" I say.

"Yeah, it really is. The stakes are pretty high for all of us."

The lights dim and then rise to settle people into their seats. Then Rob's father stands. He reminds me of Tony Soprano in size and demeanor.

"I'd like to welcome you all to what we hope will be the first of an annual event, the Pellegrini Filmmakers Competition. It was certainly thrown together in a hurry, but in this business time has no weight. As filmmakers our patience is stretched often for years as we push a project. Other times we're expected to work miracles within days or weeks. And so the first requirement for these films tonight was that they were not previously completed in production, and they've never been shown before. You'll see in your program the complete rules.

"We have a distinguished panel of judges . . ." He introduces each one to the applause of the crowd. "And so let us begin."

The first film is a story of a couple at an Italian restaurant hiding under a table during a mob hit. The man and woman see how their relationship isn't working only by this intense situation.

The second film is like an abstract painting come to life. There are no actors, no story, just an artistic rendition of . . . something. I don't know what, and the audience doesn't appear to either. There's mediocre applause, though one of the judges is clapping loudly.

Our group moves to the front row, replacing the last team. Kaden squeezes my arm as I pass him to sit a few seats down. I wish I were next to him, holding his hand through this momentous event.

Applause, lights fall. And then from the darkened screen, the music rises. Our title, *Solitude*, and then . . .

A voice.

I don't remember a voice at this part.

"We're here to view the creation of a creation. The filming of a film. The teamwork of a team."

The camera whirls and rocks, making my head dizzy a moment before SG's face appears only inches from the screen. He says, "The making of *Solitude*."

Ruby Unscripted

My mouth drops as it hits me. At the same moment, the film is shut off and the room is in darkness. Cass says, "What happened? Where's Rob?"

There's a low rumbling from the crowd. Then Rob's voice calls from the back room. "I apologize, there's been a bit of a mix-up. If you'll just hold tight a moment . . ."

A few chuckles from the audience. The room is dark again.

I feel a tap on my shoulder. "Ruby, we need you back here."

I follow Josef through the nearly pitch-dark theater. "Is it the wrong disc?"

"What do you think?"

I can barely see Rob's face in the light from the computer screen.

"Is this the only disc you brought?"

"Yes," I say. "What happened to it?"

"Oh no," Rob says and puts his head in his hands.

The room starts to move with restless feet and a few snickers.

"What's happening back there?"

"Need some help with your team, Rob?"

"This is a disaster," he says. He takes a few deep breaths, then stands. "Lights."

The lights come on, and Rob walks forward. People in the audience stare at him and whisper among themselves. I see it all from the back with Josef beside me, still trying to understand what happened. What did Sound Guy do with the real disc? Did he ruin it and then take off? But why would he do such a thing?

Rob confers with his father, bending down in front of him. I hear him whisper, "We could get the master disk and be back in thirty or forty minutes."

251

Rob's father shakes his head and whispers, then stands and announces, "Ladies and gentlemen. I apologize, but it appears that one film will not be showing tonight. Group three is disqualified. Let's go on to group four."

Team four hurries toward the projector. Our team moves awkwardly out of the theater amid the questioning gazes. My eyes meet Kaden's with a sorrowful expression. All that work for nothing.

I wait a few minutes before following them up the stairs.

Rob turns from the group. "Ruby, what happened?"

"What do you mean what happened? I didn't do any—"

"You were supposed to get the master from the safe."

And it hits me then. My distraction, how I grabbed a disk from the desk. And I remember vaguely that SG said the master would be in the safe. It wasn't SG's fault. Or anyone else's. It was mine.

"I messed up."

"You can say that again. What you do reflects on this group. It reflects on me. We're not just doing this for a hobby, for fun. Our work is our art. My twin sisters could've done better than this. And they're in fifth grade."

"Wait a minute," Kaden says, coming close beside me. "You can't put all the blame on Ru—"

"Rob," a deep voice says from behind us. His father. "Come to the house after this. We need to talk, and I have an early flight."

"I'll be there in less than an hour."

"Good."

Rob's father returns down the stairs, but his presence does not.

252

"I'm sorry." What else can I say? I can't even believe this. I've ruined our group's chance—and I really think we might have won.

Rob puts up a hand. "We'll talk about it tomorrow. I have to go." And with that he heads toward the door.

Kaden follows without a glance in my direction.

Someone calls from another film group and says, "Hey, man, don't worry. You'll have another shot."

But our team knows that for Rob, there is no other shot. We've been humiliated in front of the other groups. He's been humiliated in front of his father.

"It's okay, sweetie," Mom says, putting her arm around me. I push it away as Mac, Austin, and Aunt Jenna circle around me. And suddenly I feel like I can't breathe. After all the hard work. And with such stakes. I think of the members of my group, of their talking about "If we win . . ."

"What happened, Ruby?" Mac asks.

"Ruby picked up the wrong film," Mom whispers to him.

"So the real film isn't here?" he asks loudly.

"Yes, and it's my fault, and only mine. All my fault."

The downstairs crowd is cheering. The noise in the coffee-house heightens like the sudden turn-up of volume.

A few people mill around, glancing our way as my family circles me, consoling expressions on their faces. Mom touches my chin. "Don't be too hard on yourself," she says, and the others nod. "It was your first time doing all of this. They can't expect you to be perfect."

I want to scream at her, and then suddenly I am screaming and pushing away. "That was way less than perfect! Don't you get it? Everything I do lately is a failure. My entire life is a disaster. And if you hadn't called me right when I was picking it up, maybe I wouldn't have been distracted. You don't see the consequences of all the things you do to us."

Mom looks confused at my words, and that makes me angrier. Does she really have no idea how much she's ruined our lives?

"I hate it here. I hate that you made us come here, that you decide to change our entire lives and we have to follow whatever you want. And then you don't even see how hard it is on us."

"Ruby," Aunt Jenna says, stepping toward me. I see Mac scurry toward Austin and Uncle Jimmy, who have moved away during my outburst.

"Do you know that Mac wishes he could build a time machine and go back to when you and Dad were married? Everything is harder and different, and we just want our mom and dad to come home to. We don't want to choose one or the other. I don't want my brother living in a different town. I don't want to take turns at Christmas or . . . or . . . You and Dad ruined our lives."

And then I see the disappointment in Aunt Jenna's expression and the hurt in my mom's. But I can't stop—the words keep coming, the emotions, the tears, the feelings of despair.

"You and Dad promised to stay together. You raised us in church and taught us to put God first, then your marriage . . . and then you get a divorce? You ruined all of us. And I want to move home."

"Home?" Her voice is so quiet it's hardly audible.

My voice is easily heard by anyone around. "Yes, and don't act like you don't know what that means. It's not my fault you and Dad made our lives so hard. I want to be with my old friends at my old school."

"Ruby, we'll talk about this when you calm down."

"No. I'm calling Dad. I'm going home." And then I turn and rush through the kitchen and out the back door, knowing I should have run away before all those vicious words came spewing out. But they are truths. And I don't want to keep fighting for everything anymore. I truly do want to go home.

The cold surprises me. I'm without phone, purse, or jacket again. And where can I go anyway? No car, too far from home to walk, nobody to come save me.

Why doesn't God send a person, an angel cloaked as a human—I'll take a bum or that guy on the solar-powered unicycle. *Just, God, please send someone.*

I wish it'd be my brother.

Or my dad.

I don't want to see my mom. Don't want to hear her anger or see her cry.

If only Natasha would arrive right now.

Once again I'm sitting on a street curb. And no one comes. Which figures. Doesn't it just figure?

I mean, what does God really want from me? I give up. I give up trying to figure this out all alone. Once I dreamed of bridges, but lately all I've been doing is sitting on curbs. I get up and try again, try to be grateful, try to seek God's purposes, try to explore who I am and who I'm supposed to be. And this is where it gets me.

I rest my elbows on my knees and rest my face in my hands. Tears fall between my fingers and onto the cold gray parking lot.

Then I hear footsteps, and I know it's not my angel or anyone I want who is coming up beside me.

The scent of her perfume arrives before she does. Yes, it's Blair who sits next to me.

She laughs. Blair, the woman who only cracks a sardonic smile, is actually laughing. Laughing at me. Tears roll down her cheeks, and I ball my hand into a fist.

"I'm glad this is so humorous to you." I really might hit her. "Just leave me alone."

"You know, I haven't sat on a curb since I was probably five years old. Or maybe I've never sat on a curb. This is pretty pathetic."

"Yes, it is."

"I heard what you said to your mom. That wasn't like you at all."

"And I'm sure you enjoyed every second of tonight."

"Not really. I decided I like you though." She looks at me with a hard examining eye. "Yes, I like you very much. I was wrong about you, Ruby. But don't become like me, okay?"

"O-kay."

"Listen. Rob isn't going to hold this against you. It wasn't really your fault. He and Josef should have checked the film hours before the competition. None of us will blame you. And your mom is going to forgive you. Everyone will forget this happened, eventually."

"But—"

"I said to listen to me."

This takes me back. "Okay, but whoever you are, and whatever you did with Blair, I don't care."

She doesn't laugh at that. Then she says, "Don't think I'm going to stop making fun of you or your religion though."

"Of course not. I know you don't like anyone that much."

And this makes her laugh as she walks back toward the Underground. Who would've guessed Blair would be my angel?

I'm shivering and still considering Blair's words when Austin pulls into the parking lot. "I dropped your mom and Mac off already," he says as I get in the passenger seat.

It's a relief to be with him alone; he's good about leaving me to my silence when I need it.

Austin turns on my favorite radio station, and we settle in for the drive toward home, down the winding, hilly roads of Mill Valley. When we reach the house, Austin leaves the car idling a moment and turns the music off.

"I'm glad that I get to be your stepdad."

This makes me smile sadly, considering the disaster that I am.

"Do you want to know what your mom said about you and your brothers before we started dating?"

I don't answer, only stare toward the open garage that is still lined with unopened boxes.

"She said that some people would say she's a woman with baggage. But that if I considered her children baggage, then I shouldn't bother going on even one date. She had baggage, no doubt, but her children were not it. She said, 'My children are named Carson, Ruby, and Mac. And they are my greatest assets.' I think I fell in love with her at that very moment."

This makes me smile a little, though it also makes me feel very sad.

"I shouldn't have said—"

"Ruby, you've become an asset to my life as well. I'm grateful to be your stepdad. And except for a few things tonight, I'm very, very proud of you."

After acting like the meanest person on the planet, what do I say to that?

After a bath, I peek into Mom's room where she's in bed watching TV with Austin.

"I'm sorry," I say.

"It's okay, sweetie. We can talk about it now if you want, or tomorrow."

"Tomorrow, if that's okay," I say and then move to my room, feeling another wave of emotion trying to drown me. I was horrible to my mother, embarrassed her in front of dozens of people, but worst of all, I said the most hurtful things to her that I've ever said to anyone.

My phone rings as I sit on my bed—it's Kate's number.

"Kate," I gasp into the phone.

"I'll just admit that I've been ignoring you."

"You mean you could've talked to me?" The hurt comes through in my words, and then I apologize. And it's a "Sorry" that I need to say. "I don't blame you."

Neither of us speaks for so long that I wonder if she hung up on me.

"You there?"

"Yeah," and her voice sounds small and fragile.

I want to be there, to put on our pj's and make brownies and watch *Ever After* or *The Princess Bride* or both, like we always did when life was hard.

"I don't know what to say. Or what to ask. I don't even know what's going on."

"Yeah, I know. Let's just say that my parents found out everything."

"Everything?"

"Yes."

"Are you okay?"

"I wasn't. James won't ever speak to me again. The whole school knows what happened. It's so embarrassing on so many levels. My dad acts all awkward around me, and he told James if he came near me again, they'd put him in jail. And for a week, I missed James so badly, I seriously thought I might die. I remember your mom saying once that divorce was so terrible she thought people could die from it. I understand that now."

"I should have been there for you."

"Yeah. You should have."

Then I hear her smile—it's so weird how I can hear Kate smile.

"You can be there for me now."

"I want to come home. I'll probably come up this weekend."

"Why don't I come down there? It sounds great to get away, and Mom said she'd bring me."

"Okay." I adjust my pillows and slide under my thick down comforter. Life isn't complicated within the warmth of my bed. "I wish I hadn't moved down here."

"You belong there."

"No, I don't. I've made a huge mess of things down here—"

"Hey, you're talking to the Queen of Mess."

"True, you do get the crown for now."

"Thank you very much. But the thing is, when you lived here, there was a part of you that was bored with us."

"That's not true. I've never been bored with you."

"Maybe bored isn't right. But you weren't challenged here. You were exploring everything, not fitting anywhere."

"I don't fit with anything here—"

"Not true. You fit there in lots of ways. Not in a lifestyles-of-the-rich-and-famous way. But in the energy, the opportunities. It's your place."

"Now don't you sound all wise and mentorlike."

"I've seen a glimpse of hell and survived. My hair should be gray." She laughs a little. "It's been awful. My parents wanted to press charges, but I'm as much at fault as he is. I made my own choices. But there are good things coming out of it too. So remember that—don't think coming back would solve things for you. It wouldn't at all. I miss you and wish you were here. But you don't belong here now. You sort of never did."

Before I can decide on a response, she continues.

"I'm not going to do the things you're going to accomplish. And I don't even mind, 'cause those things aren't me. I don't need to see the world or create great works of art. But you'd just better stay Ruby Red and not get too stuck-up to go toilet-papering with me."

I laugh. "I won't, I promise."

"Good. Then no more talk about moving back. And start planning some fun things for us this weekend."

epilogue

"It's not that far of a jump," Blair says as we swing our legs over
the edge of the railing.

I stare down at the smooth surface of blue water thirty feet
below us. Kate is on my left; London, Blair, Cass, and Frankie
are in a line at my right. And for some reason, I suddenly think
of Tony Arnold. Why does the memory of a kid I didn't really
know follow me around at the strangest moments—like this one,
as I'm standing at the top of a bridge?

"It's a bit dangerous, maybe illegal," London says with a fearful glance at the water below.

Maybe it's the dangerous part that reminds me of Tony, the
idea of death. And I want to remember him. Maybe if I remember, his life will hold more meaning and remind me to make
mine more meaningful. Maybe?

Frankie scoffs. "It's not illegal. Rob got permission from the
city."

"He got *permission* for us to jump off a bridge?"

"It's sort of an off-the-record permission—the city doesn't want to get sued, you know."

"Why are we talking about this now? The longer I stand here, the harder this is going to be." Cass is mesmerized, looking downward.

"Oh my word—yes, I stole that from you, Ruby—but anyway, oh my word, women are such wusses," Frankie says, which elicits enough threats that he apologizes profusely. "Okay, I take it back. But let us all know, this is a rite of passage. My parents did this in high school. I hear about it whenever we drive out here. But their jump wasn't documented and used for a film. We're gonna be stars, girlfriends!"

Frankie waves at Rob, Kaden, and Josef, who stand on the bluff with tripod and video camera. Kaden gives me a thumbs-up and that irresistible smile. The past few nights he's been at my house, and Kate's given her approval even if she agrees he can be a little lost in his thoughts.

Rob yells, "We're rolling, so go when you feel like it."

Rob apologized the day after Film Disaster Night—as our team now calls it—saying it wasn't my fault and he shouldn't have blamed me. There was a series of mishaps that night, starting with SG writing our film's title on the "Making of . . ." version.

But I think Rob would still hold it against me, if not for the surprise from his father. After viewing the movie that might have been, his dad said we would have won the competition, and he'd try to get everyone on our team intern positions on his next film. They're working on the details, but if I can earn enough money for a plane ticket, there's a chance I'll spend part of my summer in Southeast Asia on a major film production and lounging on the beach at night.

And, of course, Kaden will be there as well.

I must admit I've spent a significant amount of daydreaming on that scenario.

The warmth of the sun today is summer's coming promise. My hands grasp the railing behind me as I get ready to jump. I glance at Kate, who gives me her loud happy smile. I see the old Kate in her face and know she's coming back to the girl so full of life and fun. And we're standing on a bridge together.

What it is about me and bridges?

"Let's do this," Frankie shouts.

"All together?" Cass asks with hesitation.

We lean forward to examine each other's faces, nodding in agreement.

"All together on three!" I shout.

Together we count, yelling and laughing. "One, two . . . three!"

And we jump.

We're in the air, falling and screaming. And for the smallest moment of time, we're each alone and yet also together, suspended in that space between bridge and water, surrounded by air.

And I guess life is just that.

Moments of living on the ground.

And also, great moments completely surrounded with sky.

acknowledgments

Ruby is a character who really came to life and brought me along a wonderful journey. So my first thanks goes to her.

To Maddie's best friends and my other "daughters"—Caitlin Clark, Natalie Martinusen (best cousin), and Morgan Holub—for inspiring the joy, excitement, and angst of being a teenager. I love you girls!

I'm grateful to my husband, Nieldon Coloma, for your solid and pressing belief in me and my writing and for loving me so. Cody Martinusen, my adventurous firstborn, you are always loved and admired, no matter where you roam. Weston Martinusen, you fill my life with wonder, laughter, and love.

My editors see more of me than I often can and guide me well. Thank you, Ami McConnell, for discoveries in my writing and pointing out the gold. Natalie Hanemann, for belief and great guidance, for seeing and encouraging. LB Norton, what fun we had editing *Ruby*, and what a great experience working with you again. And I am always, always grateful to Allen Arnold—thank you!

Kimberly Carlson, I so appreciate your friendship, our kindred spirits, and your writing support and guidance. This book was greatly enhanced by your thoughts.

To the women in my life: my mother, sister (sister power!), mother-in-law, sisters-in-law, my agent/friend (Janet Kobobel Grant), and my many girlfriends—you make me better by knowing each of you. And to Ruby Duvall: how thankful I am to know and be the granddaughter of such a woman of life, love, humor, and strength.

I mostly thank my daughter, Madelyn Rose Martinusen, for being my inspiration. This is to the beautiful, intelligent, kind, dream-filled, sparkly, best girl in the world. I love you so!

reading group guide

1. Ruby is uprooted from her hometown and moves to a town with a very different culture. Have you ever been the "new girl" in school? How did you adjust? What were the hardest things about leaving your old life behind? What were the easiest?
2. How do you cope with being alone? Are you good at making friends? If not, what are some ways to find good friends?
3. When you feel out of place, what do you do to find stability? Do you tend to make more mistakes during these times? What are ways you can overcome instability and loneliness?
4. When Ruby's best friend, Kate, comes down for a visit, Ruby struggles with balancing her old life with her new life. Have you ever experienced this? What did you do?
5. Kate makes a lot of mistakes in a short amount of time. Have you ever had a friend make huge mistakes that

damaged her life? How did you treat her afterward? Did
you have to get adults involved? Did you help her heal?

6. What are some ways to balance doing your own things,
and seeking your own purpose while retaining relationships
that aren't going the same direction?

7. In what ways can you cherish the past, work toward the
future, but stay focused and grateful in the moment?

8. How solid are your beliefs and faith in God? What are ways
you'd like to further explore growth in your spiritual life?

9. If you were surrounded by people who had a different
belief structure than you, how would you keep their
friendship but stay true to what you believe?

10. Do you believe that you can "script" or make your life
what you want it to be? How much is in your control? Do
you turn to your faith to help you with areas that are
beyond your control?

11. Do you have hobbies, activities, or interests that you feel
are your purpose or calling? What do you think is the
purpose for your life?

12. If you live in a divorced home, do you have a hard time
maintaining your relationships with both parents while
living your own life? Do you continue to struggle with
the divorce? Is there any part of you that feels guilty about
the divorce? What are healthy ways to forgive your parents
and to grow from the past?

Experience one girl's journey to rebuild herself into someone who is truly beautiful.

Beautiful

Truth's Found When Beauty's Lost

CINDY MARTINUSEN-COLOMA

THOMAS NELSON
Since 1798

AVAILABLE NOVEMBER 2009

CPSIA information can be obtained at www.ICGtesting.com
Printed in the USA
LVOW04s2308031013

355286LV00007BA/118/P